Dangerous Revelations

A Linked Series

Susan Bacoyanis

ISBN: 978-09909209-3-9

First published in 2019 by Endeavour Media Ltd.

Author's Note
Dedicated to all women who have suffered abuse.

A True Testimony
The terrible act of abuse Gilda suffers in the story is based on a woman's real life experience that I heard described on BBC Radio 4. It brought me to tears and I wanted to draw attention to the bravery and suffering of the woman who related her story.

Table of Contents

Foreward

Dangerous Revelations is the sequel to *There Are No Accidents* and continues my Linked Series.

*

Previously, in Los Angeles:
"I'm asking you to write my biography. I can assure you that I have enough material to hold your interest... you won't be bored," Gilda told her.

*

Frances obtains a journal at auction, which helps her write a biography of the late Lauren Carter who was murdered while she was married to Gilda's son Gary. Frances is living with Tom, the detective who is responsible for Gary serving a thirteen-year sentence for Lauren's murder, which he didn't commit.

When Gary is released from prison, he goes looking for revenge and stalks Frances. Tom needs help to stop Gary and contacts a Mafioso he met at Gary's trial. Subsequently, Gary is murdered by the Mafia and Tom is wrongfully accused by the LAPD — and so he flees to Italy, to hide among his Mafia friends.

Frances is totally ignorant of Tom's link with the Mafia and plans to join her partner in Italy. Before the trip she meets Gilda, who bid against her at the auction for Lauren Carter's journal. During the meeting, Gilda requests that Frances write her biography, but Frances is noncommittal. After lying low for six months, Frances joins Tom in Italy, but soon realizes the horror of their new existence...they're living within the Mafia *Family*, from which there seems no escape.

Frances cleverly convinces the godfather, Dino, to let her visit LA to complete a commissioned biography, with the promise to return. During her journey, she switches her connecting flight to Geneva, where she's met by Gilda. Inside Gilda's home, she sees a photo of Gilda's husband and mistakes it for Dino, the godfather. Frances is terrified by Gilda's connection to the Mafia and collapses with fright. Gilda comforts Frances and explains that she was married to Dino's twin brother and offers Frances permanent refuge from the Mafia.

Frances is relieved and agrees to stay with Gilda in Geneva, to write her biography.

Geneva Awakening

Day One

My eyes were open, but I was not present. The morning sunlight was angled through the wooden blinds, disfiguring the interior of my room. I lay in a subliminal state, unaware of time and motion. Then, quite suddenly, I felt the rush of consciousness flood my mind and I knew I was alive.

I heaved myself up from the bed and struggled to recover my equilibrium. I walked towards the huge French windows, flung them open and leaned out over the wrought iron railing. An unabashed fresh breeze chilled me and a vortex of air carried chattering voices from the street below. The language was not my own; German, perhaps? The aroma of coffee and sweet pastries caught the updraft and I remembered… I was in Geneva. A new day had dawned. I was alive, safe and hungry.

A knock at the door preceded the entrance of the housekeeper with warm towels and freshly-squeezed orange juice. I thanked her, showered, dressed and made my way down the two flights of stairs.

"Good morning my dear. I hope you slept well."

"Like a baby," I replied.

"Good to see you looking refreshed," Gilda said. "Come, let's have some coffee before we begin." I followed her into a brightly-decorated room, which she referred to as "the day room". There, we devoured Viennese pastries and enough coffee to alert me for the task ahead.

"This is to be our work room," she said, gesturing with a circulating hand action. "It's my favorite room, so full of light. I think we're going to need this uplifting atmosphere to balance the dark side of my life story."

I looked at her compassionately, wondering what horrors I would encounter. She caught the mood of my gaze and spoke quickly to reassure me.

"Don't worry my dear, you're a strong woman, you can handle it."

After breakfast we moved to a space by the window. Gilda made herself comfortable in an armchair, while I set out a notepad, two pens and my laptop upon an antique desk, inlaid with leather and gold. I switched on my digital voice recorder and held it on pause.

"Are you ready, Gilda?"

"Yes," she said, clearing her throat nervously.

"The Book of Revelations… day one."

I began recording and together we embarked on an intrepid journey into Gilda's past.

*

My mother, Lia, was Italian and Jewish. My father, Carl, was not. He was of Austrian descent, which was the only thing he had in common with Hitler. He and my mother were very much in love and planning a fine wedding, when my father received an official letter.

He approached his parents to break the news. "I have something important to tell you, please sit down." He tried to prepare them for the words they'd been dreading. "I've received a letter," he said and handed it to his father.

"You've been conscripted into the army," his father read aloud.

"Oh no, this can't be?" His mother was upset.

"I refuse to serve under Hitler. I abhor Nazism… I'll never be a Nazi," he told them, taking a stand. "I intend to leave Austria immediately."

"Will you follow your brother to America?" his father asked. "You could take a passage on a ship from Naples, as he did."

"No, I've left it too late to get to the ports. The Italian route is already crawling with Nazis," he said.

"Oh my dear, what about your wedding?" said his mother.

"I've obtained a special marriage licence," he said, "I'm sorry mother, but Lia and I leave tonight."

"Then you are in God's hands now," his father said.

"It breaks my heart to leave you both… will you come with us?" Carl said.

"No my son, we'd slow you down…we're too old to travel and hide. We'll stay and face the consequences… whatever they may be." His father placed his arm around his wife and spoke for both of them.

"Come back to us…" his mother's words were drowned in her tears as my father kissed them both goodbye and none knew if they'd ever meet again.

A few hours later, my parents were secretly married, before they fled Austria to begin a new life in Holland. The year was 1937.

*

They settled in Amsterdam, in the safe home of my mother's cousin Gina. She'd married a Dutch man, Hans, and both worked in the diamond and gold industry.

"We're both academics," my mother told Gina. "We know nothing about gold or diamonds. Except that a diamond is the hardest naturally-occurring material."

"Well, you know about the structure of a diamond," Hans said, "and gold—"

"Gold is a chemical element... symbol AU and atomic number 79. It's a transition metal and a group 11 element," my father reeled off his knowledge of chemistry.

"And its melting point is 1,064 C," my mother added her bit of knowledge, too.

"Well, it seems you know more than most," said Gina. "We'll teach you the business and you'll soon become experts. We're happy to help you. God knows, we all need help now."

"The Jews hold a monopoly in the gold and diamond industry here in Amsterdam, but things are changing." Hans paused and shook his head in disbelief. "They're leaving. It's due to the rise of fascism... it's sweeping across Europe and the wealthy Jews are emigrating to America and Palestine."

Gina placed her hand on Hans' shoulder to calm his distress.

"The Jews who remain are in imminent danger. They're either in denial or they can't afford to leave," Gina added.

"Each family wants to protect their livelihood, but they may lose their lives."

"I underestimated the speed of this enforced segregation," said my father. "We have to keep Lia safe."

"I know how to do that," said Gina. "Lia will immediately become a Catholic... you both will."

My mother's cousin had married out of the Jewish faith, for which she'd been ostracized by the rest of the family. She'd married a Dutch Catholic and had integrated into his community. My mother had stayed in touch with Gina since childhood. They'd remained close and formed a loving bond which served her well, as now she too had married out. Ultimately, this would save both their lives.

*

The year was 1940 and Amsterdam was a dangerous place in which to live.

"Lia, have you heard the news?" Her cousin had looked terrified. My mother called my father and they gathered to hear their perilous future.

"The Germans have invaded the Netherlands and they're heading directly for Amsterdam," Gina said.

"Then this day, May 10, 1940, will be recorded in history as the beginning of the end of the Jews."

My father's words were profound, and within a short time his prophecy came true. The Jewish businesses were doomed… and so were the Jews. One hundred and twenty-eight Jews who resided in Amsterdam committed suicide during the first week of the German occupation.

For my parents, survival meant new identities. They changed their last name. My mother and her cousin became sisters on paper and my father was given the identity of a Dutchman, who'd died suddenly, before his time. My mother now displayed a gold cross around her neck, a crucifix hung in each room in the house and both attended Mass on Sundays.

"How do I look?" Lia had asked.

"Unrecognizable!" said my father, observing my mother's newly-lightened hair color. "And those eye glasses… they hide your beautiful dark eyes. At least I can remove them in private," he said tenderly.

"To all the non-Jewish Dutch, we are a close Catholic family running our own business. We're known in the district as insignificant, small-time traders, which is a good thing. We don't want to draw attention," said Hans.

"From now on we all speak only Dutch. Practice until your accents are perfect. Our lives depend on it," Gina instructed.

It didn't take the Germans long to begin their discriminating procedures. Jews holding bureaucratic positions, legal and educational jobs, were fired. All Jews and Jewish enterprises had to be registered. My parents' transformation fooled the Germans and thank God, they were not included in the segregation and discrimination. But their Jewish neighbors were.

"It's like watching a slow death in real time," my father observed.

"The Jewish economy that built this city is being destroyed. Their livelihoods have been shattered and now they're doomed to live in the Jewish Quarter of Amsterdam," said Hans.

"I feel so guilty," said Lia, dropping her head in shame.

"If we take a stand against the Germans, we'll be condemned. We can't fight this alone. Our job, Lia, is to survive and tell the story."

My father, Carl, was realistic.

*

As 1941 loomed, it brought with it the beginning of the demise of the Jews. Winston Churchill's words echoed across the English Channel. "Never give in. Never, never, never." My father struggled between the urge to fight and daily survival.

Tensions were growing as the Dutch Nazi organizations were targeting the Jews in their allocated Jewish neighborhood.

"There's a new group of Jewish and non-Jewish supporters. I'm joining them tonight. Come with me, cousin?" Carl pleaded. "We're going to help them fight back against the Nazis."

There were several nights of battling in the streets of Amsterdam and both my father and cousin were injured.

"My God. look at you both. You're bleeding. Quick, Lia, lock the door," Gina ordered, as they helped the two men inside. "Into the kitchen... we'll tend to their wounds here. Fetch some hot water from the stove, Lia."

They sat my father and Hans by the stove and patched them up.

"The last battle resulted in the death of a Dutch Nazi."

"I didn't know that some of the Dutch joined the Nazi movement!" Lia said.

"They're labeled... turncoats. They're scum," replied Hans.

After that night, the Germans sealed off the Jewish Quarter, as it came to be known and non-Jews could no longer enter.

One week later, there was another incident. My father and Hans were not involved.

"There's been a massive fight in Koco's, the Jewish ice-cream parlor. It's reported that the grune polizei tried to enter and were confronted by the Jewish self-defense unit." As Hans relayed the news, tears formed and tricked down his cheeks.

"The Nazis took their revenge." He paused and wiped his face. "They sent four hundred and twenty-seven young Jewish men to Mauthausen concentration camp."

"Let's pray for them," said Gina.

"They'll need more than our prayers," said my mother. "They'll need a miracle."

That was a decisive moment for my father. He joined the Dutch Communist Party. He, along with his comrades, organized a general strike to be held on February 24, 1941. It was ostensibly meant to show the Nazis that their persecution of the Jews was economically too costly.

"You must join us," my father had told the Dutch workers. "Solidarity is our only hope. We'll squeeze the Nazis where it hurts… in their pockets, bank accounts, convenience stores and public transport, and through our lack of cooperation we'll beat them down."

My father was one of their leaders, and on February 25, the public transport workers were the first to strike. The communists spread their strike manifesto across the city, encouraging others to join their cause.

"We've paralyzed the city and it's only noon." My father had been ecstatic. But there was a heavy price to pay for disruptive disobedience.

"Listen… can you hear the sound of engines?" said my father.

They listened for a few seconds. "My God, look!" said Hans, pointing to the street corner.

"Turn back, turn back!" My father and Hans turned around and frantically waved their arms at the men following them into the fight.

"Turn back… run. We haven't a chance!"

Hans and Carl forcibly tried to stop their men, but the protesters heard only their own battle cry… and they roared blindly ahead and into the arms of the German military police.

"Carl, hurry, get inside the house!" Hans pulled him through the door and locked it. The two men raced upstairs and watched the street from an upstairs window.

"I want to fight alongside them," my father complained. "I feel like a coward."

"We wouldn't survive," said Hans. "The protesters haven't a chance against the Nazi force."

"Listen, there's a rumbling noise and it's louder than the previous engines… quick, it's getting closer," said Hans, "follow me."

The two men rushed up to the top floor of the house and threw open the window. From their vantage point they could view both ends of the street.

"I have to stop them!" My father began yelling, as more protesters advanced from the south end of the street.

"It's too late—"

A concentrated artillery bombardment blocked the width of the street at the north end and began firing on the protesters.

"We have to do something—"

"No, we'll be killed and we have wives to protect," said Hans.

The German military police brutally repressed the brave protesters. Those that lived were seized in the streets, thrown into trucks and never seen again. It was a massacre. Apart from the strikers who were killed in the street, many were also severely injured.

When the battle was over and military police retreated, Hans and Carl went to help those were left to die of their wounds. The local Dutch community lifted the injured into their houses and helped others to a hospital.

My mother and Gina had been stranded on the other side of town. Rumors were circulating about the massacre. One person told them that several strike leaders had been executed by firing squad, and my mother was terrified.

"Carl! Thank God you're safe!" Lia dissolved into tears as she entered the house.

Both women were overcome with tears and gratitude on realizing their husbands were safe.

"You're injured?" my mother said, looking at the congealing blood on my father's arms. You too, Hans."

"Get upstairs and we'll clean you up," said Gina. "If the Nazis come to check, we all need to be accounted for… quick!"

My mother scrubbed my father down, patched up his wounds and dressed him in clothes that concealed the bandages. She then helped him down the stairs and they all settled into chairs in the front room… and waited.

Within half an hour, they heard the inevitable knock on the door.

"We've come to take a census, due to the uprising," the German soldier said as he pushed his way into the house. "It states that there are four of you living here, correct?" He counted heads. "Two men, two women."

"Just my sister, myself and our husbands."

"Catholic family?" the German soldier interjected, pointing to the large crucifix hanging above the fireplace.

"Yes."

"Me too," he said. "Haven't seen my family for a while, I miss them." His sentimental moment was brief. Then he clicked his heels, "Heil Hitler," he said and left them in peace.

A few days later, the Germans made an announcement.

"I fear the worst has happened," said Hans. "We have so enraged the Germans by the men striking and helping the Jews, that they've taken further retribution."

Gina, along with my mother and father, listened intently as Hans read the report sheet handed out to every household.

"It is stated that the German High Command has declared the Jews enemies of Germany and whosoever aids them will suffer dire consequences."

"Carl, you have to leave the Communist Party," pleaded my mother. My father reluctantly agreed.

During those few days after the uprising, a further three hundred men were rounded up and immediately sent to Mauthausen, where they later died.

My parents and their cousins kept a low profile and no one suspected that my mother was Jewish. The Germans commandeered the Jews' gold businesses and formed a syndicated gold center, for which they appointed Aryan administrators. My parents were among the chosen few. The irony… my father and my Jewish mother were working for the Nazis! It was unbelievable.

*

"Frances, I'm tired. Let's take a break," Gilda said.

"Of course, Gilda," I replied. "But your story has stirred a childhood memory of mine. I recall hearing my parents talking about the Dutch uprising, but I can't remember why. I was too young to gather the context of the conversation, but I distinctly remember that it was about someone in our family."

"Ummm, interesting. Perhaps my revelations will reveal your past, too," Gilda said with an uncanny air.

I shuddered, as goose bumps ran up and down my spine and I recalled that Gilda had spoken of this once before.

"Well my dear, there is more drama to come," she said.

I just smiled. I knew this book would develop into an extraordinary saga.

*

I didn't arrive on the scene until the spring of 1947. My mother had been too frightened to conceive a child during the occupation and besides, the Dutch were almost starving. The Allied liberation brought more than personal freedom for my parents. It brought the prospect of wealth. Now that the Germans had been defeated, the gold businesses were to be returned to their rightful owners… the Jews of Amsterdam.

But the Jewish community had been almost completely wiped out. More than one hundred thousand Jews, had been deported during the war and the diamond and gold trades had virtually disappeared. Except for those businesses assigned to Aryan managers, who'd been forced to control the gold trade to enrich the Third Reich. My parents had been key controllers of the German gold trade in Amsterdam, and their claim to inherit their business was justified.

"Lia, I searched for the prior owners, but they're gone. The whole family went to the camps… they were all wiped out," said Carl, after searching the survivor records.

Lia looked at him with tears in her eyes, "Then we as survivors, will carry on," she said, placing her hand on his shoulder.

"I almost feel guilty we're alive," Carl said.

Lia looked her husband directly in the eye. "Remember my dear, I'm Jewish. If either of us should feel guilty, it's me… and I'm not going to let guilt destroy our lives."

"You're right Lia, we will bear testimony to the atrocities," Carl stated.

"And there's another reason," said Lia. "Together, we are creating the next generation."

"You're pregnant?"

"Yes, I'm three months gone," Lia said, smiling at her husband through now joyful eyes.

They told me I was their Golden child, so my parents named me Gilde, which means golden in Dutch. I later anglicized it by changing the last letter and from then on I was Gilda.

I grew up the only daughter of two very hard-working individuals who taught me their trade. I learnt how to estimate the value of gold, make jewelry and the fundamental principles of building a successful business. Study and hard practical work consumed my childhood. I spent hours listening to my father negotiate business deals. After school, I hung around his workshop, watching, learning how to use the tools and practicing the delicate, detailed art of jewelry-making. At thirteen, I was proficient and at fifteen, I was an expert and fulfilling orders. They were wonderful, intelligent and loving parents. I am eternally grateful to the God who chose these human beings as my life givers.

*

"Now, shall we have dinner Frances, before I emigrate?" Gilda suggested.

The American Dream
Day Two

It was 1964 when my parents announced that they had decided to sell the business and emigrate to America. I was seventeen. The war had taken its toll on their health and they were old beyond their years. They'd worked hard to successfully rebuild their business and it was time for a change. I chose to accompany them and embraced the idea of a new life outside war-torn Europe.

Our passage to New York was on a large ship with countless others, seeking a new start. The sea voyage was fraught with storms and the ship heaved and dipped through thirty foot waves.

"Papa, are we going to survive the voyage?" I'd asked him.

"God didn't spare us for nothing. His plan is for us to live in America… and so we shall." His words were convincing.

"Hold tight, Gilde," said my mother, as the ship's bow dipped once again before the onslaught of water.

My parents had placed me between them and we'd linked arms, with my father's other arm holding a rail.

"I feel sick, can I go below?" I said.

"No, you'll have to lean over the side. We must stay above the water line. The hatches might burst under the pressure of the water, then God help the folk below decks." My father was adamant.

Just as one storm ended, another seemed to flare up and I was sick for days. When we eventually arrived I was thin and frail, due to my immense weight loss.

"Gilde dear," my mother said, "we're approaching the port of New York. Would you like to catch your first glimpse of the Statue of Liberty?"

"I wouldn't miss it for the world," I answered. "But I'm so weak."

"Come Gilde, your mother and I will support you," said my father.

They took hold of each of my arms and the three of us made our way to the uppermost deck for the spectacle.

"She's magnificent," I said.

"She's a majestic figure of a woman, Gilde… just remember you're a woman too. If ever you should need to be brave in your life, remember this sight, on this day."

My mother's words sustained me over the years and I revisited the vision of that icon at key moments in my life.

There was a hush among the passengers as all gazed in awe upon the statue.

"God bless America," someone shouted from the crowded deck below.

"God bless America," was the unanimous reply. Then a rapturous roar encircled the ship. Everyone was cheering and throwing their arms in the air. We had arrived safely and the feeling was euphoric.

My father had decided that we would spend two days in New York to prepare for our overland journey.

"Papa, this is the longest and biggest car I've ever seen," I said, surveying the used Cadillac before me.

"It will accommodate the three of us and our luggage. We've a long drive to Minnesota," my father said.

My mother stopped in her tracks when she saw it. "It's hideous!" she exclaimed. "Carl, you can't seriously be thinking…"

"It's a necessary purchase dear," he replied, winking in my direction.

My father leaned towards me and whispered. "Umm, by the look of distaste on your mother's face, I don't think it will remain in our possession too long." And then he laughed. It was so good to see them happy.

*

We set out for Minnesota and navigated our way across the United States. The few larger items that we'd decided to bring from Amsterdam were following in a container ship and they'd be trucked to our new home later that month.

Our journey was an education in itself. I'd never been outside Holland and now I was traversing a continent. It was unlike anything I'd encountered before and I soaked up every image, sound and odor… even though some of the farm smells were offensive.

We were travelling north to greet the cold, and we were totally ill-equipped for the extreme winter weather. But Minnesota was my parents' choice and it was where we would put down new roots.

*

My parents' choice of state was based on the recommendations of friends who had emigrated during the previous years, and where my uncle had first settled. They chose a small town outside the city of Minneapolis, where they bought a traditional town house and planned to live happily ever after. There was enough money for me to attend college, so when I turned eighteen, in 1965, I anglicized my name and enrolled at the University of Minnesota, where I began an exciting, independent life within the Minneapolis campus.

"You have a talent for languages, Gilda," the principal had said. "And you've had the advantage of living in Europe. You'll be one of our fast-tracked students… we're pleased to enroll you."

I shook his hand and enjoyed meeting my professors and fellow students. Some of the girls suggested I join them. "Come with us tonight Gilda, we're going to a bar," they said.

"I thought drinking was off limits until the age of twenty-one?" I replied.

"No one cares about that… so, will you come? There'll be boys," they said.

I turned them down. I was naive… I'd had no experience with boys and besides, I wanted to build a good reputation. This was my chance to succeed academically at something I wanted to do. I worked hard during my first year and eventually I began to socialize, too. But I was discerning regarding the company I chose to keep.

"Gilda, you're always studying. Don't you ever have fun?" Dr Allen, one of my professors, had asked.

"I enjoy my studies, professor," I answered politely.

"All work and no play makes for a dull girl, you know," he said.

This was not the first time he'd approached me in the library. But on this occasion, he let his hand rest on my shoulder and lingered longer than before.

"I can feel your clavicle, Gilda. Your bones are not fleshy with fat and you look hungry. Ummm… I think perhaps I should take you to dinner," he said.

I think I was flattered… and so I agreed to have dinner with him.

We began to dine regularly and formed a friendship, until one night he proposed a change. "Gilda, I'm becoming very fond of you. I'd like us to form a more serious relationship," he said, taking my hand and stroking it.

"Are we talking sex?" I asked boldly.

"Yes, you sweet girl, but if you prefer, I could say it romantically. Gilda,

I want to make love to you. I want you to feel utterly and completely uninhibited in my arms. I want you to abandon all thought of your work and come to my bed. And I want it… tonight."

His words overwhelmed me and again in my naivety, I thought I was special.

I thought he loved me… although he didn't say it. Like a lemming, I rushed to my destruction.

In other words… I went to his bed.

I was unsophisticated, immature and vulnerable. He overwhelmed me with his powerful personality and superior knowledge and so it was during my first semester of my second year that I fell in love.

Every month, I would return home to visit my parents, whose lives seemed set in a regular pattern. Three times a week they'd walk a mile to the local town to have coffee and pastries in the Viennese patisserie. They'd always sit at the same table in the bay window, eat their sugary treats and read the European newspapers.

On one such morning, about a week before my planned visit, they followed their usual routine — but the roads were icy. Not that this deterred them; they'd endured worse things in life than a little ice. They sat sipping their warm coffee, watching the flutters of snow fill the sky.

On this particular morning the soft snow was falling on frozen ice, disguising its treachery. Outside, an articulated truck transporting heavy farm equipment skidded and the vehicle jack-knifed. The driver tried desperately to control the truck as it danced across the ice, spinning the cab and its contents in opposite directions. As a finale, it lanced the protrusion of the bay window in one clean cut, aligning it to the other existing architecture. The bay window, its seating and my beloved parents… all were gone.

*

"Please sit down miss," the police officer had asked politely. A female police officer sat beside me. "I have some bad news. I'm so very sorry to inform you… that your parents have been killed."

I remember that moment as if it were yesterday. My heart was beating so fast I thought it would explode in my chest. But strangely, time seemed to slow down. I began to ask how… but the words wouldn't form coherently.

"It was a tragic accident and I'm afraid, as you're their only living relative, you'll have to identify the bodies," he said.

"But why? You already know it's them, "I protested.

"It's a formality... I'm sorry," he said.

The female police officer took my hand to comfort me. "Do you have a friend who could accompany you?" she asked.

I decided to ask the man I loved to share this awful task, but he insisted he had an urgent appointment for which he apologized... a little too profusely. So I went alone.

Standing in the morgue, I kept thinking of my father's words during our perilous voyage:

"Gilde," he'd said, "God didn't spare us for nothing. His plan is for us to live in America." "But Papa, I whispered, "God didn't say for how long."

*

"Frances, I need a break. Even now, thinking of this makes me so sad." Gilda paused and let a tear escape. The retelling of the incident was agonizing and haunted her once again. "Forgive me, I still feel their pain," she said.

Words would have sounded inadequate, so I leaned forward and gently placed my hand on hers.

After a brief interval and some refreshments Gilda regained her composure.

"Frances, I'm ready to move on with the story now," Gilda said, donning a brave smile.

*

I was only nineteen years old when the accident happened and I was unprepared for my parents' deaths. I imagined they'd live happily into their old age... they certainly deserved to, after their heroic survival in war-torn Amsterdam. But life throws curve balls, and this one hit me fair and square where it hurt. We think we're invincible until the unthinkable happens. But after the agony and grief, there was the prospect of life after death. I just had to find it.

I attended to the necessary procedures with guidance from the local church. I was raised a Catholic, but I'm drawn to the Jewish faith, which is my birthright. In Jewish law, a child's bloodline is derived from the mother. So technically, I'm Jewish. You know there was a rumor that Hitler's mother was a Jewess? I've always seen the irony in that. I often wonder if there was a huge maternal problem in his life... possibly an

17

Oedipus complex, which he resisted. Maybe that's the fundamental reason he hated the Jews? Of course, it's complete conjecture on my part.

The people in the town were kind, but my parents had kept to themselves, so there were no close friends of theirs to support me and I felt totally alone.

I now owned a town house and had inherited their retirement fund. I was financially comfortable, without external concerns. I chose to concentrate on my last two years of study and used that and my boyfriend as a distraction. The reality was too hard to bear.

My professor approached me with an idea. "Gilda, I too have experienced the death of my parents, but their demise was less traumatic. Because we're both alone... I was wondering if we could accelerate our relationship to a more serious level? I'd like to move in with you."

"I wasn't expecting us to live together."

"Darling Gilda, I'm fifteen years older than you. I want to make an honest woman out of you."

"Are you proposing marriage?" I asked.

"No... not exactly, but in time," he replied.

"Well, I hadn't intended to live with you unless we became engaged," I said.

"And we will... in time."

"You've never even told me you love me," I stated. "Why would I live with a man who didn't love me?"

"Gilda, of course I do!"

"Is it so difficult for an educated professor to say those actual words?" I was beginning to feel upset. It didn't feel right. I'd convinced myself some time ago that I loved him.

"I love you. There, I've said it. Are you happy now?"

"I love you too... but you know that, because I've told you on numerous occasions," I said.

He was my first love. I was nineteen and he thirty-four. I misread his declaration of love because I was needy. A cold loneliness had chilled my heart and I needed someone to warm it. He was kind, compassionate and available. It was easy to love him, so I'd let him into my heart and now, into my home.

We lived together until the month of March in my final year. Even then, during the late swinging sixties, living together was quite avant-garde.

*

"I'd been blissfully happy, Gilda said."

"Don't you mean *we*?" I suggested.

"No, sadly I was the only one in the relationship who felt love, and I was too young to realize that he was playing games behind my back. There were rumors circulating the campus. Rumors of his aggressive sexual behavior towards the students, but I chose not to listen. I thought these women were exhibiting jealousy. I was blinded by my love and inexperience."

*

Then, like many naive girls, I fell pregnant. In those days there was no instant test. So I kept my secret and waited three months until the doctor confirmed my pregnancy. I was overjoyed at the news and eager to share my happiness with him. I arranged a special evening, just for the two of us. I cooked some good food, dressed prettily and waited for him to come home.

"What's the occasion?" he'd asked, seeing the candle-lit dinner I'd arranged.

"I have something wonderful to tell you… I'm pregnant," I proudly announced.

"What? You stupid girl."

"I thought you'd be pleased…"

"Get an abortion," he ordered.

"How could you consider an abortion?" I said. "You'd be killing your own flesh and blood!"

"Gilda, watch my lips," he said getting into my face, "If you don't get rid of it, I'll end our relationship right now."

I pleaded with him to give it some time. But he flared up in anger.

"You bitch! You set out to catch me," he said. "Well I won't fall for your little game!"

"What are you saying?" I said. "I thought we intended to get married?"

"Marry you? Never… you're nothing but a slut," he said… and then he struck me across the face. "You think I don't know you've been sleeping around? This child could be anyone's."

"I would never…"

"Slut!" he shouted again.

My cheek was still stinging from the first blow, when he hit me once more. I protested my innocence. I was crying hysterically because

19

I'd done nothing wrong, but he wouldn't listen. He stormed into the bedroom, stuffed his clothes into a bag and left.

He was no more than a bully. I remember sitting down on the top stair as he slammed the front door. I had thought that after he heard about the baby, we'd be celebrating… we'd get married. But I was too young and ignorant to understand men like him, men who use young girls and then discard them. He gave me no more thought than an old pair of shoes whose soles were worn through. I was devastated.

*

"Gilda, let's get some air," I suggested.

But she was unresponsive and lost in this sad memory. I watched her and waited patiently. She was holding her cheek and smoothing it with her palm as if to alleviate the physical pain of his abuse.

After a minute or two, she smiled and we walked in silence down the stairs and into the kitchen, where we shared some fresh lemonade.

"Gilda, are you sure you want to continue?" I asked.

"Of course, Frances," she replied. "It's just that I'm reliving the emotions… silly really, as it was so long ago, but to me, they feel like yesterday."

I squeezed her hand and when she was composed, we returned to our work.

*

I tried calling him for two days, but to no avail, so I drove to the university to make my presence felt. The staff knew us as a couple and I wanted them to know about the baby. I wanted to tell them that their professor was going to be a father, with parental responsibilities. I wanted to shame him into acceptance. After I'd spread the news, another professor took pity on me.

"Gilda, I think it's about time someone told you the truth," she said, walking me into her office and closing the door. "You're not the only woman who's fallen prey to this professor. There have been many complaints regarding his sexual advances towards young women, particularly from freshmen who were too scared to pursue legal charges."

I was stunned. How had I not known what seemed to be common knowledge around the campus? At first, I was in denial.

"You must be mistaken. We're obviously talking about different people," I asserted.

"Professor Allen?" she said

"Yes, Michael."

"Correct," she said. "Sadly, I've dealt with this man before. It was concerning one of my own students with whom he'd been having an affair. This young pregnant student had confided in me and disclosed that Professor Allen had given her money for an abortion. She was a Catholic and when she refused to get rid of the baby he became so enraged that he punched her in the stomach and then pushed her down a flight of stairs."

"Was the girl alright?" I enquired.

"She lived, but as expected, she lost the baby. She tried to press charges, he denied everything and blamed the student for provocative behavior. He insinuated that her injuries were inflicted by a fellow male student. Nothing was ever proven."

I was so shocked. I couldn't believe that she was talking about the same man... *my* man!

"Gilda, has he hit or abused you in any way since you told him about the baby?" she asked.

"Yes," I admitted.

"Then would you be brave enough to pursue charges against him?" she asked.

"Yes but, we were alone and again it would be his word against mine," I said. "I think I'd lose."

"You know, I'll support you if you change your mind," she said sympathetically, and handed me a sheet of paper. "Here are some organizations that may be able to help you... good luck."

I left her office and stood with my back against a stone wall. Tears welled up in my eyes and I wanted to scream out loud... *it's not true...* but it was, and I had to accept the fact I had just become another statistic, added to that national list of unmarried mothers-to-be.

Shortly after that conversation, Michael left the university.

*

"Let's take a five minute break," I suggested, and Gilda agreed. I was impatient to hear more, but I realized that these breaks were necessary when extracting highly emotive material.

After a while I asked a question. "Gilda, when I first arrived in Geneva, I remember you telling me that your first husband, Gary's father, was a criminal. But, now you say you were an unmarried mother?"

"Yes, you're correct. I told you he was my first husband, and that I was a young deserted wife in a foreign country, with no home, no money and a newborn baby. I'd lived with the stigma all my life… I wanted to make a good impression. Remember, I didn't know for sure that you'd write my biography. Now, of course, I can be honest. Won't you forgive me Frances?" she said.

"Of course," I replied. "I completely understand the difficulties of that era."

*

Now, where was I? Oh yes… I tried to compose myself that afternoon. I waited calmly until Michael exited his class — and then I confronted him. To begin with, he just laughed and dismissed my words as a malicious rumor propagated by a jealous lesbian… referring to the female professor. This was absurd and it made me angry.

I tried again to extract the truth and this time he became consumed with rage. He swore at me and called the campus security to have me removed. I accompanied the new guard to the gates, who informed me that he'd heard about the professor's party trick, from his former colleague. Apparently, it had happened on several prior occasions and he kindly suggested that I'd be better off without him.

I boxed up the remainder of his belongings and left them outside my home for him to collect. I locked the door and watched as the father of my child callously abandoned us. He walked out of my life as effortlessly as he'd entered it, leaving behind a memory and his genes.

I thought I'd never see or hear from him again. But there was a further blow to come, which seriously impacted my life.

*

About a week after Michael left, I had a call from my bank informing me that I hadn't enough funds to cover my expenses. If you remember, I told you that I'd inherited my parents' retirement money along with their town house. I used a savings investment account to provide me with an income and apparently, I had transferred the balance to a joint account in both my name and Michael's. In disbelief, I went directly to the bank manager and there in black and white was a form with both our names and signatures.

"That's not my signature," I'd told the manager. "I've never seen this form before and I demand to know who certified this transaction."

I was furious. But at first, they didn't believe me!

"I want you to summon the employee whose name is on this document," I told the manager.

A young woman appeared.

"Do you know who I am?" I asked her.

"No, I don't believe we've met."

"Then how is it that you witnessed my signature on these documents?" I challenged her.

She turned to the manager and fumbled her words.

"Speak clearly, Miss Jones. Did you, or did you not, witness this lady's signature on these documents?" The manager asked.

"Well no, not exactly…"

"Then what exactly *did* you do?"

She then confessed that I'd not been present at the formal setting-up of this joint account. "He told me that you were gravely ill in hospital."

"Who told you?" the manager was becoming impatient.

"Dr Allen," she said. "I was told that he and his wife needed to establish a joint account to pay the hospital bills. Dr Allen was distraught. He broke down and cried, right here in the bank. He said — and I remember his exact words — that the mother of his child was fighting for her life and not expected to live. He said that a joint account was crucial, to ensure future ease of finances, particularly for the child. He implored me to let him sign for both of them… just that once, as time was critical. I thought she… you… were dying!" The bank clerk was panicking now.

"And did you let him sign both signatures?" asked the bank manager.

"I felt so sorry for him… and in the circumstances I thought… well, I thought it would be alright." The bank clerk turned to the manager for a sympathetic response.

"Clearly, you *didn't* think! You coerced a criminal to commit fraud, a crime," said the manager.

He immediately called security, who came and took the clerk away, then made a call to the bank's fraud department. Then, the manager and I sat and completed insurance claims.

It was now a criminal investigation. I went to the fraud department at the police HQ to make a statement. They contacted the university and were told that Dr Allen's tenure had been terminated and the college was not aware of a forwarding address.

Back in 1968, before we had global communications, it was much harder to trace someone. Michael had simply disappeared. I was three months pregnant. I had no income, no husband — but I had a house. If necessary, I had something to sell.

Soon after, I received a lump sum from the bank's insurance company, which enabled me to stay in the house throughout my pregnancy. In theory, promiscuity was all the rage in the 1960s, but it was different in real life. There was still a stigma attached to young girls giving birth out of wedlock, particularly in Minnesota.

*

"Gilda, why is it that throughout history, women seem to have been punished for having sex?" I asked.

"It's because men and women have always been held to different standards," Gilda said. "Even in 1968, men were encouraged to *sow their wild oats,* whereas single mothers were considered socially unacceptable."

"I'm not sure much has changed," I said.

"Yes, it's very disappointing. Let's eat," she suggested.

And so we ended this sad episode with the thought of a good dinner and much-needed glass of wine.

Life After Love
Day Three

In the spring of 1968 I turned twenty-one, and in the May I took my finals with my five-month bump wedged against the desk. I was ostracized by most of the staff and students for blatantly displaying my pregnancy around the campus. In spite of all my setbacks, I later graduated as a linguist. We spoke Dutch when I was a child. I already knew some Italian, French and German from my parents and I learned English in school. I found languages easy to acquire.

In September, I gave birth to a baby boy and I named him Gary. The name is derived from an old Germanic word, meaning 'spear'. Somehow I thought it would give him strength throughout his life — and maybe it did. But I also gave him my grandfather's name, Lionel, meaning 'lion', which symbolized courage.

"You thought most carefully about his names," the doctor commented.

"I know they'll travel through life with him. I have nothing else to give," I said.

"Do you have any family or friends to support you?" he asked.

"Not one. I'm totally alone," I told him.

"You're a very brave young woman," he said.

But I wasn't. I was terrified! Oh, how I longed for my mother.

My confinement had been overseen by a staff of cold-hearted nuns, who disapproved of my morals and reminded me daily that women who live loosely don't deserve to be mothers. I was advised to place my baby for adoption immediately after giving birth.

I remember the stern expression on the nun's face as she coldly handed me the papers to sign.

"Your son will be placed with a childless couple of impeccable moral standing. He'll be raised a catholic and they will pray to God for his grave sin," the nun lectured.

"How can a baby have committed a grave sin?" I questioned.

"He is illegitimate," the nun said, "born out of wedlock… and that is a sin."

"But that's not his fault—"

"That's for God to judge, not you," preached the nun, with a steely expression.

I was so enraged by her words that I've never forgotten them. They've haunted me throughout my life. It's silly, I know, but I look back and see how he turned out and I wonder... what if I'd kept my baby?

But common sense prevailed. I knew I wouldn't be able to work and although I'd received some insurance money, my inheritance had been stolen and in all probability would not be recovered. If I placed my child up for adoption, he would likely have more opportunities; a good education, a two-parent family... I wrestled with this decision and eventually made my choice.

I chose to give him up.

In life you never get over the painful events, as people often suggest. But in time they become a little easier to live with.

*

"Gilda, I don't believe in God's wrath," I said. "I think the nun just wanted to scare you."

"Yes, of course you're right my dear," Gilda replied. "She was very unkind."

*

Two months had passed since I'd parted with Gary and the bite of the November weather was setting in. I'd applied for several jobs that would take me to warmer States, where I could begin to lead a new life. My adjustment to normality, as if that really exists, was slow, and one evening I let my guard down. There was a knock at the door; I ran downstairs and blindly answered it without checking.

It was Michael.

He pushed his way past me up the stairs and into my home.

"I've come to see my son," he said.

I was stunned. "Last time we spoke you denied ever *having* a son,"

"Last time we spoke *you* were the problem. I didn't want to get tied down... but now I want to see him."

"He's *my* son, not yours. You gave up all parental rights when you left me. I went through the pregnancy and birth... alone."

"So? I've changed my mind." He leaned forward to kiss me and I pushed him away. "Huh!" he laughed. "Playing hard to get now, are you?"

His behavior repulsed me. I walked to open the door at the top of the stairs. "Get out!" I said.

"Gilda, silly girl, didn't you hear me? I said I want to see my son."

"You can't. He's not here."

"I'll wait," he said.

*

Gilda turned towards me. "Frances, I want to explain what Michael was like. He was a sociopath with narcissistic traits. His inflated idea of his superiority and his high IQ meant he thought himself smarter than everyone else — and that was his downfall. He had the typical criminal mindset... they always think they're too clever to get caught. But they are delusional and they are very dangerous."

She continued...

*

"You stole all my money," I reminded him. "How did you expect me to bring up a child? I was broke and alone. He has new parents now."

"What?" He screamed into my face. "Gilda, what did you do?"

I began shaking and it reflected in my voice. "I gave him up for adoption."

"You had no right!"

"I had every right!" I shouted. "I was the only legal parent!"

His complexion turned sanguine and he began to rage. I hung on to the open door and hesitated... I should have run but my feet were glued to the floor. He grabbed me, dragged me backwards and slammed the door. He called me degrading names and as I tried to stand up, he knocked me down. I screamed for help. He told me to shut up and hit me across the face.

Blood was now pouring from my nose and I went into shock, crying hysterically. I was hurting and he just gloated. I remember looking at his face and realizing with horror that he was *enjoying* the violence. This was not the man I knew. Or perhaps the truth was that I had never really known him.

I tried to roll away from his grasp and struggled to my feet, only to be knocked down again. I was terrified. I screamed out for help once more, but this just served to exacerbate his violence.

We were in the living room, on the second floor. He turned, walked towards the window and tried to open it, but the catch was locked. I tried to scramble to my feet in an effort to escape, but he grabbed my legs and pulled my body backwards. He was a large, strong man and I, only a hundred pounds. I really didn't have a chance.

What came next is as vivid today as it was all those years ago. He plucked me off the floor and in one swift action he threw me against the large picture window. I heard it crack and as I tried to lunge forward, he kicked me back against it… and this time, it broke.

And I fell from the second floor.

I remember falling. It was as if time had slowed down. I looked up at the night sky and my last view was of the stars.

I believe an angel was watching over me, as I landed on a carpet of snow and it saved my life. But I couldn't move. I had no pain. I thought I was dead. Thoughts of my baby boy raced through my mind and then… nothing.

*

"Gilda," I said, noticing the tears cascading down her cheeks. "Let's stop for a while."

I placed my hands on hers as they lay clutched together in her lap. They were wet from the tears that had rained upon them. She looked up at me with an expression of agony that was indescribable. Words failed me, so I leaned forward and cradled her in my arms. Pain seemed to radiate through her frail body and I felt that if I squeezed too hard, she would disappear.

Gilda had shared her moment of desperation with me and I felt ashamed of those times in my life that I'd complained about minor incidents. Her pain was infectious and the two of us sat and cried together.

Gilda decided the point at which to resume, which we did later and after some refreshment.

*

I survived by the grace of God and the hand of an elderly neighbor. His name was Eli and he'd known my parents.

He found me on a white pillow of snow, decorated with my own blood and just before I froze to death. He gently covered me with his coat and went to call 911. He then returned, layered me with blankets and sat rubbing my hands in an attempt to prevent hypothermia.

Eli's statement to the police described how he was initially disturbed by the noise of raised voices. He then heard my screams and, thank God, he ventured outside and found me lying in the snow amidst broken glass. If he hadn't heard, I'd be dead.

I was in hospital for four months. The carpet of snow was just thick enough to save my life, but not to prevent multiple broken bones and internal injuries. These, according to the doctors, meant that I'd be unable to have more children. But worse than that, I had no recollection of the incident.

Eli was a widower and he visited me almost every day. He was a holocaust survivor and it was his strong survival instinct that instilled in me the will to live. I remember thinking that if he could survive Auschwitz with all its horrors, I could survive too.

He gave me a purpose to live for… it was revenge.

*

"Gilda, the name Michael Allen is playing on my memory. Did he become famous?" I asked.

"*Infamous* is the best word to explain why you've heard of him. He was murdered."

"Oh yes," I recalled. "It made headline news… but I can't remember when."

"The year was 1997 and I was fifty years old." Gilda's expression changed to one of hatred, as she relayed the information. I wanted to ask her the obvious question and she read my thoughts.

"Yes, I did take my revenge, but that comes later." Gida's facial expression lightened with a gentle smile. "Hungry?" she asked.

I nodded.

"Good. Let's eat lunch."

*

I was at the point of giving up, but I knew I had to reclaim my life. Everything I'd loved had been taken from me and I'd lost the will to live. Eli had physically and mentally saved me and with his help I slowly recovered my memory. First, I began to have flashbacks of that dreadful day. Eli patiently encouraged me to connect my flashbacks and I began to remember everything. He was there to soothe me when I recalled the horrors, and when I awoke from the nightmares which accompanied this conscious awakening. I owe him so much.

He explained the mental exercises he'd developed to outwit the Nazis.

"Gilda, always remember that your strength is in the mind," Eli had said. "They could starve and humiliate me in Auschwitz, beat my body to a pulp, but they couldn't get inside my head… unless I let them.

I was a conscious human being and my thoughts were my own, so I instructed myself to stay alive. It was for one purpose… revenge. If none of us survived the camps, who would testify to our persecution? I was determined to bear witness to that evil. There are those who deny that the camps ever existed. But I know… I was there. And until my dying day, I am a living proof of their lie."

Eli's eyes were wet with tears as he spoke of his terrible ordeal. He took my limp hand in his and instilled in me the will to live.

"You are witness to this terrible deed caused by an evil man," he told me. "You must will yourself to mend, so that one day you can track him down and take your revenge. Your task, my dear, is to hold him accountable for this abomination."

He also reminded me who I really was.

"Gilda, you're Jewish, like me," he'd said. "We believe in an eye for an eye and a tooth for a tooth. It is written… his punishment must fit the crime."

He was in earnest.

So, I worked my mind and my body and I began the slow process of recovering from my harrowing experience and Eli was there every step of the way. After four months in hospital and one month recuperating at home I had grown mentally and physically strong, and I was ready to reclaim my life.

But some things would never be the same. I'd have to live with some permanent bodily damage, scars seen and unseen and without the hope of children. But I would live… and that was enough.

*

"Gilda, did you pursue charges of assault against Michael?" I enquired.

"I tried. But my statement was delayed due to amnesia caused by the shock. It was several months after the event that I regained my memory and was able to recall the sequence of events. The police investigated the incident, which took place in November 1968, before the permissible use of DNA. So there was no real evidence," Gilda explained. "Just my scars."

"But surely they questioned Michael?" I said.

"Briefly, but he dismissed their questioning with his usual air of superiority; he the elite professor and I a mere student of twenty-one. He rebutted my claim, insinuating that I was traumatized after the death of my parents and that I had psychological problems which led to bouts of drinking. In those days... I didn't stand a chance."

"So he just walked away and you had no way of obtaining any recompense or damages?" I was stunned.

"That's correct. I couldn't afford an attorney. If the police could have accessed the communication methods we have in place today, no doubt they'd have found him guilty. But in the late 1960s things were very different," Gilda told me.

*

My hospital bill was horrendous and I realized I'd have to sell the house to pay my debts. At that time I had no idea where I would live, or whether anyone would employ me. My stamina was low, but my mind was recovering and my will to regain a life was open to a challenge.

My dear friend Eli once again came to my rescue. He had some long-standing friends in New Jersey who owned a jewelry business. They were a Jewish couple in their early fifties and they had a vacant position for a live-in apprentice.

It was something I could do immediately. I still had some brain fog, which prevented me from seeking a high-powered job using my recently acquired degree in languages. The doctors told me it could take up to two years before my concentration levels were restored. Apparently, the brain functions better with a known, previous skill that is ingrained, rather than a relatively new accomplishment. My dexterity was good and because I grew up in the jewelry business I knew it inside out. I also needed somewhere to live.

It was a godsend and I didn't hesitate. I placed the house with a realtor and flew to Atlantic City, New Jersey. Eli agreed to oversee the house sale so I could begin a new life as soon as possible.

*

My arrival was met with great warmth. Neta and Mendel Wolff opened their home and their hearts and I found a place in both, a safe haven in which to rebuild my life.

I learned from Eli that sadly, they'd lost their only daughter three years before. She was engaged to be married and Neta and she were busy planning the wedding. Their daughter had been visiting the dressmaker, for a final fitting of her wedding gown, when two Mafiosi from opposing New Jersey Mafia families had a confrontation in the restaurant next door. The shots exploded — first from inside, and then the men tumbled out onto the street. There followed random shooting from another patron and the Wolffs' daughter was caught in the crossfire… gunned down in the street two weeks before her wedding.

I knew I could never replace their daughter, but my presence brought them comfort. I'd had a quieter existence in Minnesota and was totally naive about the east coast. I soon realized that Atlantic City life was very different from Minneapolis. It was controlled by the Mafia and they fleeced every business.

*

"Gilda, there has been a lot to absorb today," I said, observing her exhaustion, but pretending the burden lay with me.

"Yes, I too feel emotionally drained. I think I'll rest this afternoon," Gilda replied.

I watched her as she climbed the stairs and marveled at the inner strength of this fragile-framed woman and the roller-coaster life she'd lived.

Atlantic City, New Jersey
Day Four

"Good morning Frances. How did you sleep?" Gilda asked as I joined her for breakfast.

"I went out like a light," I said. "I haven't slept so soundly in years."

"It's the air. There's nowhere quite like it and that's precisely why I made Geneva my home."

"Gilda, are you finding our sessions emotionally difficult?" I tentatively enquired.

"I believe that the blood and sweat of a life is felt in the soul, and only from the soul can one perceive its true meaning," she said.

"Those are profound words," I replied. "But the process is painful."

"It has been my privilege to experience pain and joy in my long life. If we don't experience pain, how can we appreciate joy?"

"I understand."

"Now, let's talk about life in Atlantic City, shall we?" Gilda said.

I followed her into the day room and our work began.

*

Mendel and Neta's jewelry business had a shop front on the main street. The workshop was at the back with a separate entrance. Above the store was their home and now it was mine, too.

My room was large and feminine; it had belonged to their daughter and was decorated with wallpaper of pink roses. It had become a shrine after her death, and not until my arrival had any other person slept in her room or in her bed.

Neta, a small, slender woman with graying hair, walked me into their daughter's room.

"It's been a long time since I heard sounds of life from this room," Neta told me, "but I need to move on and you are welcome in our home Gilda."

"Thank you, I'm so pleased to be here. I'll work hard and help you with household duties too," I assured her.

She nodded in agreement. "Mendel will show you the workshop in

33

the morning. Breakfast is at seven and we open the shop for business at eight-thirty. You'll soon get the hang of everything." Neta smiled at me, studying my undernourished body. "After you've had a wash and unpacked, come on down for dinner... seems you need feeding up, and I'm a good cook," she added kindly.

That was the beginning of my new life with Mendel and Neta, who were to become my adopted parents. We each had wounds that needed healing and a vacuum that the other could fill; mother, father, daughter. They treated me like a daughter and I grew to love them very much.

Mendel was small in stature, with sharp features and a nose that dominated his face. His hair was graying too, just like Neta's but unlike her husband, Neta had soft features with a round face and small nose. I remember thinking how well she'd have passed for a Dutch Catholic back in Amsterdam. My work bench was adjacent to Mendel's. After a week, Mendel approached me.

"Gilda, I've been observing your skills and your craftmanship is excellent," he said. "I'd like you to handle all the repairs and resizing."

"When I worked with my parents I used to design jewelry and take commissions," I told him. "Perhaps I could do that for you?"

"I'll consider it," he said.

I'd been working hard for a month when he called Neta into the work shop.

"Close up the shop Neta and let's gather around the table. I have some business to discuss. Gilda has proved herself a talented craftsman. I understand that she used to design jewelry and take commissions. I think now is the time for her to organize a catalogue of her original designs," he said. "Neta, do you agree?"

Neta agreed.

"Oh, thank you Mendel" I was exuberant and threw my arms around him.

"It will expand the business," he continued, "give us a chance to keep more of our money."

Before he could finish, there was a knocking on the shop door.

"We're closed," I said. "Who would be knocking at this time?"

Neta looked directly at Mendel. "It's the end of the month," she said.

Mendel's facial expression changed and he became solemn.

"Alright... I know who it is. You both stay here." His tone was adamant. I looked at Neta to explain, but she hung her head low and stared at the floor.

"What's happening? Why do you look afraid?" I asked.

"It's him," she said. "He's come for our money."

"What money? What's going on, Neta?"

She looked at me with sad eyes, took my hand and softly explained. "Every month we have a visitor and we hand over protection money."

"Protection against *what*?" I asked.

"Against the very people we're paying."

"I don't understand!"

"They're Mafia, Gilda. They demand a percentage of our profits and if we don't pay, then… they'll ruin our business." Neta looked distraught.

"Oh my God! That's awful… that's against the law. Have you called the police?"

Neta laughed. "The police have been 'fixed'. That's what they call it in New Jersey."

We heard Mendel locking the shop door and he joined us.

"I've told her," said Neta. Mendel took the bottle of bourbon from the dresser and poured himself a glass. After a sip or two he seemed calm enough to talk.

"We're living in a swamp," he said. "Our state is controlled by the New Jersey Mafia. Half of what we make…" he shook his head in disgust, "goes to them. They run an extortion racket and call it a tax. In exchange, they give us their assurance that no harm will come to Neta, myself or our business."

"I can't believe it!" I said. "It's outrageous, it's immoral."

"It's the end of us, if we don't pay," said Mendel, draining his glass.

I felt helpless. The only thing I could do was to work hard and try and increase their off-the-record income. I began sketching several designs; necklaces, bracelets and dress rings. Mendel had them printed in a small catalogue which he kept in the window to attract customers.

*

It was now 1970. Things were going well and I was happy. A year had passed since I moved in with Neta and Mendel and I grew stronger, thanks to their love and care. I was well fed and healthy and I didn't need outside stimulation. I had a family again and that was enough. I took my share of the house chores and the cooking, but Neta always prepared the food on the Sabbath.

In those days, I no longer believed in God. It didn't matter to me which religion I chose. I was technically Jewish, because my mother was an

Italian Jewess. To survive in Amsterdam, we all passed as Catholics, and that was my childhood religion. But Neta and Mendel kept the Sabbath and I enjoyed sharing this tradition with my new family. Every Friday night, Neta would prepare the supper and Mendel and I would race to finish our work before sundown.

Over the next six months, I worked hard to increase their sales. But then, one particular Friday evening, our routine changed.

"Gilda, my child, enough working today," Mendel kindly stated. "Quick, go and wash or Neta will have our hides!"

"Just one more…"

"No. God rested on the Sabbath and so do we," he said.

Neta was lighting the candles, and Mendel was just about to recite the blessing, when there was knock on the shop door. We all froze. Mendel and Neta shot each other a knowing look.

"It's not the end of the month until next Tuesday," she said.

The knocking continued and it was getting louder. Mendel discreetly peered around the connecting door. "It's him."

"I'll go," I said. "It's the Sabbath."

"No, Gilda."

"I know where the bag of cash is. Please, I insist."

"Let her go," said Neta. "We will pray."

I walked through the shop, switched on the lights and unbolted the main door. "Please come in," I politely asked him. "I'm Gilda, I live here."

The dark-haired Italian Mafioso smiled and followed me into the shop. "Where's Mendel?" he asked.

"He and Neta are beginning their supper," I told him. "It's the Sabbath."

"Don't you eat?"

"Yes, but I'm Catholic," I said.

"Me too," he said. "My family's Italian."

"My mother was Italian too." I tried politely to find some common ground.

His face softened and he smiled. "I'm Benito," he said. "I'm known as Beni." He put out his hand.

"Gilda," I said, taking it. "Have you come for the cash?"

"Yeah, I know it's earlier than usual, but we've got a…"

He stared at me for a few seconds and then changed his words. "I'll be away next week," he said.

"It's alright, I have the cash," I said. I paid him and hoped he'd leave immediately.

He nodded respectfully and deposited the wad of cash into his inside jacket pocket. "You're very pretty Gilda," he said. "Hope you don't mind…"

I shook my head and thanked him for the compliment. Then I opened the main door and wished him good night.

"You handled that well Gilda. It helps us that he liked you," Neta said.

"How does that help us? He's Mafia!" Mendel replied, challenging his wife. "You think because of Gilda's pretty face, they're going to stop collecting?"

"I don't know… maybe," said Neta. "Gilda, do you think he's handsome?"

"Yes," I replied. "He's more than handsome… he's a devil in a cloak… that's an expression my mother used. She was always suspicious of handsome men, said they were trouble." I laughed.

"He's trouble alright… he's Mafia! How much trouble do you want?" said Mendel, shaking his head.

"It's just fun talk, you old fool," said Neta.

Mendel threw his hands in the air, "Aye yai yai," he muttered.

"But I love you." She smiled at him with a face full of love. His anger dissolved and his expression instantly softened. The strength of love between them was almost tangible.

I soaked up that moment with delight, but oh, how I wanted just one look like that in my lifetime, from someone I truly loved.

*

Gilda smiled, but only her lips moved. Her eyes shadowed her feelings of sadness.

"Gilda," I said. "Let's return for a moment to God. You said that you no longer believed in God. Can you tell me why?" I asked.

"Everyone I loved had been taken from me; my parents, my child and my lover. When I was young, I couldn't understand how God could inflict so much pain. So I cut him out of my life."

"How do you feel about God now that you're older?" I asked.

"I believe God gave me consciousness and a brain by way of a tool to apply my intelligence. I have lived my life by utilizing my wit and wisdom. Both have served me well."

"You've certainly had an interesting life. I look forward to hearing more," I said.

"Huh… You ain't seen nothing yet," she said. "That's a quote of Ronald Reagan's."

"Yes, I know that one!" I said and laughed.

*

Soon it was the last day of the month again. Mendel counted out the money for the Mafioso to collect.

"We've had a prosperous month, thanks to your speed of work, Gilda," Mendel said.

"I'm pleased to contribute," I told them. I'd worked hard to increase their sales.

"We'll only bank the regular amount. The Mafia have the banks in their pockets. If they see from our deposits that we're banking more profit, they'll demand more," Mendel said. "Neta, hide this somewhere safe." He handed her the extra cash.

Mendel stopped and listened. "That's him knocking. Quick Neta, take it!" He waited until she was out of sight, then he walked to the main shop door.

"Come on old man, open up, I'm freezing my balls off out here," Beni shouted.

Mendel open the door and the first person Beni encountered was me.

"Oh excuse me! I wouldn't have said that had I known you were here, Gilda,"

Mendel shook his head and went to fetch the cash. I smiled, "You're forgiven."

Beni's eyes were glistening as he stared at me and I knew there was an attraction. "How you been?" he asked.

"Okay, just working hard," I replied.

"So what d'ya do?"

"I work with Mendel, repairing jewelry," I told him.

He took my hand and turned it palm up. "Working hands… so where you learn this stuff?"

"I grew up in Amsterdam, where I learned the business from my parents," I said. "That was before we emigrated to America."

"So many questions," Mendel muttered under his breath.

"So why aren't you working with your parents now?" His probing was intrusive, but I answered obediently, so as not to cause a problem.

"They're dead," I told him.

Beni looked embarrassed and began to mumble. "I'm sorry."

I just nodded and left him with Mendel in the shop.

"I didn't mean to upset her," Beni said to Mendel. "She's a nice girl."

"Yes, she is and a good worker too," Mendel replied.

So that was my introduction to the Mafia. Over dinner I mentioned that Beni seemed a pleasant person.

"Mendel," said Neta, "it's time you educated Gilda, before she goes soft on the devil in the cloak."

"Educate me about *what*?"

"About the Mafia. This Beni might appear cute, but beware Gilda… they're all brutal," Neta said.

"Get your coat Gilda, we're going for a walk," said Mendel, pulling on his warm jacket and hat.

We walked up the main street and Mendel stopped in front of a shop. "You see this place, Gilda? Its frontage is all shiny glass."

I nodded.

"They pay through the nose to keep this in one piece. Look over there," Mendel said, pointing to a store with one window covered over. "My friend Alf tried to reduce the payment… they broke his window." Mendel walked on to another place. "This belongs to my friend Joe, but it's managed by his son-in-law. Can you guess why?" I shook my head.

"Joe's in hospital with two broken legs. The Mafia smashed his legs to a pulp, when he tried to snitch to the Feds," Mendel said.

"How did the Mafia find out and why didn't the Feds stop them?"

"Because the Mafia fixed them. They pay off the cops and the Feds." Mendel looked distraught. "*Now* do you understand?"

"Yes, I do. It's awful." I looked across at another shopfront, which was completely boarded up. "What happened to them?" I asked.

"They were closed down. Their profits dropped and they couldn't pay, so they…" Mendel couldn't speak. After a minute, he swallowed hard and composed himself. "They disappeared one night and…" He couldn't say any more.

I had noticed two guys across the street who were watching us, so I discreetly nudged Mendel. He tipped his hat in their direction, took my arm and steered me home.

"Who were they?" I asked, as we entered our home.

"They were Mafia Associates, they work with the Mafia… you know, report back to them. They get paid for watching the neighborhood."

"Why?" I said, "It's pretty quiet out there at night."

"They're watching out for foreign gangs who try to infringe on their territory. This protection racket brings in big money. They know who I am, that's why I acknowledged them."

"But they don't know me," I said.

"They probably think you're my fancy woman," he said with a chuckle. "Being Italian, they'd approve of that."

"Well, Neta sure wouldn't!" I replied.

*

"Gilda, for once we've ended the day on a lighter note." I said.

"Yes, Frances, I was happy at this time in my life with my new parents."

Befriending The Enemy
Day Five

Our fifth day of recording began with breakfast on the terrace, accompanied by strong coffee and Viennese pastries.

"Breakfast with you Gilda is the best… but I'll get fat if I eat these delicious pastries every day," I said.

"I used to worry about that too, but then I realized that life is too short to restrict pleasurable treats," she replied.

The knowing look on Gilda's face made me wonder just how short her life would be. But I refrained from probing. No need to spoil a perfect morning.

"Ready to begin?" I asked, switching on my voice recorder.

"Ready for some romance?" Gilda replied, smiling. "Let's go!"

*

As the end of each month came around, so Beni became more lovestruck. He'd strain his neck to look beyond the shop and into the work area. He'd ask after me. He'd linger, trying to make light conversation. He was driving Mendel crazy.

"I thought he'd never leave," Mendel complained to Neta.

"He's sweet on Gilda," Neta replied.

"What shall we do? If we prevent him from seeing her, he may turn against us."

"We have to condone it, but without encouragement," said Neta. "We have no choice."

"I'll talk to her—"

"What about?" I said, overhearing his remark.

The couple looked uncomfortable and suggested we sit around the kitchen table, as we always did when important subjects were to be discussed.

"Gilda, it's about Beni," Neta began. "He's smitten with you."

I immediately interjected to save them embarrassment. "I know," I said. "I've been listening from the back room. What do you want me to do?"

"I think it best you avoid him. We could say you were out of town."

"No," I replied. "The Mafia could easily find out you were lying. Besides, I'd have to hide away, possibly for weeks."

"Gilda's right. Best not to provoke him, just stay in the back when he collects," said Neta.

"When he calls next, I'll go upstairs and stay there until he leaves. Agreed?" I suggested.

We all agreed, but each of us felt uncertain that this would work. Least of all me.

As the end of the next month came around, we were anticipating Beni's visit. Neta heard the knock first.

"Upstairs," she ordered and I ran to my room. Mendel shut the door to the workshop and slowly walked to greet Beni.

"Hey old man, you're getting slower," Beni said, pushing his way inside the shop.

"My knees ache with rheumatism. Some days I can hardly move without pain," he told him.

"So, let Gilda bring the money," he said. "I never see her any more… where is she?"

"She's working, always working. We're lucky to have her," Mendel replied.

"Does she have a boyfriend?" asked Beni.

Mendel was taken aback by this question. "No, I told you… Gilda's always working. She doesn't have time for boyfriends." He quickly handed over the cash and walked to open the door.

"Tell her I asked after her," Beni said. He seemed irritated and looked towards the workshop.

"I'll tell her," said Mendel holding the door wide for Beni to exit.

Mendel quickly locked up and switched off the lights, just in case Beni came back. He was unusually quiet during dinner that night and I knew the session with Beni had not gone well.

*

The following week, I walked into town alone. I began to feel goose bumps on the back of my neck and I sensed someone was watching me. A car was hugging the curb-side a few feet behind me. As I turned to look, a black sedan accelerated and stopped just ahead. I froze on the sidewalk. I was shaking… I thought I was going to be abducted.

The car door opened and a tall dark man climbed out and stood before me. He smiled, removed his sunglasses and called my name.

"Gilda, can I give you a lift?" Beni said.

I couldn't reply. I was still shaking with fright.

"What's wrong?" he asked. "You're shaking!"

"You frightened me," I said.

"But it's *me*," he said, opening his arms wide.

"I thought I was about to be abducted," I answered, searching his eyes for a denial.

"Gilda, sweet girl, I never meant to frighten you. Truth is, I've missed seeing you and I thought this would be a way we could get to know each other. Come on, I'll take you for some coffee and some cake. You need sugar."

I was faced with a dilemma. If I didn't go with him, he'd take offense and I knew the repercussions could bring dire consequences.

"It's really good to see you Gilda," Beni said as he directed his driver to a coffee shop in town. "So, you like cake?"

"Yes," I replied.

"Good," he said. "Me too."

As we arrived at the coffee shop, the manager rushed to greet Beni. "So good to see you Signor Sorrentino," he groveled. "I have the best table…"

"We'll sit over there," said Beni, pointing to a table in the back corner. "And we want cake. D'ya like chocolate, Gilda?"

I nodded. "Make it chocolate cake," he ordered. "With frosting."

The staff were in immediate attendance and without delay a coffee pot and jug of cream arrived, and two enormous slices of chocolate cake. I couldn't believe I was sitting with a Mafioso!

"Eat," he said, "You need the sugar." He smiled. "Although you're sweet enough," he added, then "… just my little joke."

I was still shaky, but I forced myself to act as normal. I smiled, took the initiative and began a conversation.

"So have I discovered your weak spot?" I asked, pointing to the cake.

"I think you know it's not the cake," he said, looking at me in earnest. "I want us to get to know each other."

I looked directly into his eyes. I had to determine if he was genuine. "Alright," I said. "Where shall we start?"

"Thank you, Gilda," he said and reached across the table, placing his hand on mine. "I want to know all about you. Please start at the very beginning."

I sat with Beni for over an hour, describing my childhood and our emigration to America. I told him how my parents had died and a little about the abusive relationship.

"Tell me his name… I'll kill him," he said.

Beni's reaction was normal for a jealous man. But he was no ordinary man… he was a Mafioso. He literally meant it!

"I'd never let anyone harm you," he said.

It was quite touching to have this good looking man, whom I'd just met, eager to protect me. I continued my story and explained why I was in New Jersey. But I never told him that I'd had a child. That would remain my secret.

He described his immediate family and how his parents had brought him here from southern Italy when he was a young boy. He explained in detail about loyalty being the most important factor in his life. He talked about his family with affection and I began to see the man and not the Mafioso. He was funny, too, and I remember enjoying his sense of humor and admitting to myself that I liked him more than I'd anticipated.

After about two hours, Beni drove me home. When we pulled up outside the shop, I saw Mendel anxiously standing by the door.

"Don't worry Mendel, we just had coffee," Beni said, opening the car door for me. "I saw her in the street and I couldn't resist asking her to join me."

Mendel's face was like thunder. He looked at Beni and then back at me. "I was worried something had happened to you Gilda," he said. "Particularly after our daughter…" He choked on his words.

"I'm sorry, Mendel," Beni said with a look of compassion. "It won't happen again."

Mendel just hung his head and nodded.

"Thank you Beni, I enjoyed today," I said.

"I'll arrange things better next time," he replied, bobbed his head towards us and drove away.

I hugged Mendel and we walked into the shop together. Neta was waiting and she demanded an explanation, so I told her that Beni had stopped to offer me a lift and that I was too petrified to refuse him.

Neta put her arms around me. "I know how it is," she said. "We'll talk about how to handle this problem, but first this old man," she said pointing to Mendel, "has been pacing the shop and now he needs a drink. Actually, we *all* do."

44

"I'm not sure what we're drinking to," said Mendel as he lifted his glass.

"We're drinking to… peace of mind," suggested Neta.

"Peace of mind," we all said, as we raised our glasses.

*

Gilda paused and turned to face me. "Frances, those words were not to be taken lightly. They depicted how we wanted to live our lives… how we *should* live our lives. I began to silently plan how I would achieve peace of mind for my dear new parents."

After Gilda's serious interlude, she continued her story.

*

A few days later Beni called at the shop.

"It's not the end of the month!" Mendel said, looking worried.

"I'm not collecting today. I've come to see Gilda," he announced. "Please call her into the shop."

"She's working—" Mendel tried to stonewall him, but Beni insisted.

"I won't keep her long," he calmly interjected.

I'd heard his voice from the workshop and walked out to meet him. As I approached he quickly groomed his hair with his hand, as men do when they want to make a good impression.

"Hello Gilda." He was nervous and complimented me. "You look beautiful today."

"Thank you Beni," I said.

Mendel just turned away and shook his head.

"I've come to ask if I could have the pleasure of taking you to dinner?"

"Thank you Beni, I should like that very much," I said, without a moment's hesitation.

Beni was immensely pleased with himself. "Thank you Gilda. I'll collect you at 6:30 tomorrow then," he said. He looked to Mendel for approval, but found none.

I still remember that anxious look on Beni's face. He was genuinely afraid I'd turn him down. But of course, I had no choice.

"Gilda, out the back, now!" said Mendel. "Neta," he shouted. "We have a problem!"

Oh, was Mendel mad! He ranted and raged about my consorting with the Mafia. I told him that I knew what I was doing, but it took strong words from Neta to calm him. I suspected even then, that Neta knew I

45

had a plan and she didn't oppose me.

"Neta, she's just made a date with the devil!" Mendel said.

"So I understand," she replied. "Are you afraid, Gilda?"

"No, I'm not afraid. Don't worry Mendel, it'll keep the peace," I told him and gave him a kiss on the cheek.

So the next evening I put on a pretty dress and high-heeled shoes and waited by the shop door. Beni was on time. As I approached the car, he handed me a red rose, which I accepted. I took that as a sign of his genuine attraction.

*

"And you, Gilda? Were you attracted to him too?" I enquired.

"I was, but I kept my guard up. Dating a Mafioso was something I had to learn how to do... and it wasn't going to be easy."

*

Beni took me to a large Italian restaurant on the far side of town. When his car pulled up, the driver opened the door for me and Beni offered me his arm. I felt like a million dollars. No man had ever treated me like this before.

Beni had good manners and was respectful to the people we encountered. When we walked into the restaurant the owner rushed forward to greet us, as happened before in the café.

"Signor Sorrentino, what a pleasure to have you and your bella signorina as our guests tonight!" the owner groveled. "Your table is waiting and everything is arranged."

I wasn't sure what he meant until we entered a private dining area. It was decorated with flowers and there was music. "Beni! This is beautiful," I told him. "Is this room exclusively for us?"

"Yes Gilda, I don't want to share you with anyone else... at least for a few hours," he answered. "Do you like it?"

"I do. Thank you Beni," I said.

"We have our privacy so we can talk, but later, if you like, we could join some friends of mine."

He took nothing for granted. He was so eager to please. Oh and the food... I'll never forget it. We had freshly-made pasta with lobster and fine wine... and then two different gelatos, which we shared. It was perfect.

I offered a taste of my gelato first, which he took straight from my spoon and then he did the same for me. It was our first intimate moment and my first real romance.

Life had changed in the sixties. Romance was out of vogue. Men like Michael and guys of my own age didn't engage in romance. Those men treated me like an object. Beni was different. He made me feel like a woman for the first time in my adult life. He was a little older and of course, he was Italian. I soon came to learn that these traits are innate.

When I was a student in the sixties, we marched for equal rights and called ourselves feminists. As young women, we reveled in the idea of feminism; equality was our right and I believed it... until I fell pregnant. That's when I discovered that women were *not* equal to men, and neither were all women considered equal. Unmarried mothers were looked down upon, even in 1968.

So back to my date. Beni was smart and decent enough to explain his predicament. "Gilda," he'd said, "you're obviously an intelligent woman... you have a college degree. That wasn't an option for me. I had to stay within the *Family*. My father died when I was seventeen and my mother became ill and died soon after. I had an obligation."

"To the Mafia?" I asked, quite boldly.

"Yes Gilda, to the *Family*. Let me explain. We practice a code of conduct and loyalty, it's called Omerta."

"I understand family ties, but couldn't you have left the Mafia after your parents died?"

"No Gilda. I can *never* leave. I am bound by blood," he told me. "Family and Mafia are one. It is a strong bond."

Surprisingly, this information didn't scare me. On the contrary, I found it enlightening and I knew I could achieve my goal.

"Thank you Beni, for your honesty," I said.

"You're very special, Gilda. Building trust is our way forward," he said.

We took a long time over dinner, as Italians do, talking and laughing. We enjoyed each other's company and I discovered that Beni was well read and knowledgeable about many subjects. It was refreshing. Once we'd finished, we went to join his friends. I later learned they were all Mafia.

I'd not socialized with people my own age for a long time and I'd missed that enthusiastic zest for life. I had fun.

When we stopped outside the shop, we sat a moment in the car and Beni paid me another compliment.

"Gilda, I was so proud to show you off to my friends," he said. "Please say you'll come out with me again?"

"I will Beni," I said. "Thank you for a wonderful evening."

I thought he might kiss me, but he did something far more romantic. He lifted both my hands to his lips and kissed each tenderly, while looking directly into my eyes. It was a magical moment.

*

I noticed that Gilda was smiling into space and so I suggested a break.

"Gilda, that's quite as story," I said. "But romance doesn't cancel out the reality of his being a Mafioso."

"No, Frances, you're right. But I liked him and it made my decision easier," she said.

"And what was that?" I asked.

"I was about to strike a deal… with the Mafia."

*

Beni and I began to date regularly, much to the disgust of Mendel.

"Neta," he'd said, "Perhaps we could introduce Gilda to our late daughter's fiancé?"

"Impossible," Neta said.

"Why impossible?" Mendel challenged.

"He got married!" she told him.

"What! So soon?" Mendel said. "How could he be so disrespectful?"

"Mendel, it's almost five years since…" Neta still couldn't say her daughter's name without a surge of desperation. "People have to move on with their lives."

"Oy vey… why a Mafioso? And he's a goy? There are plenty of good Jewish boys. Gilda could have her pick!" Mendel was bemused.

"She has her reasons," was all Neta revealed at that time. For she had an inkling of the true nature of my plan.

The Deal
Day Six

It was December 1970 and Beni and I had been dating for six months. On Christmas Eve, Beni took me to dinner at his brother's house. When we arrived, I had quite a shock. I thought I was seeing double. The man who opened the door was the splitting image of Beni.

"Merry Christmas," said his brother. Then he caught sight of my expression. "Beni, you didn't tell her, did you?" He extended his hand. "I'm Dino, Beni's twin brother and yes, we're identical. He likes to play games." He gave his brother a friendly jab in the ribs.

I seriously could not tell them apart. I had to rely on their different clothing.

"When we were young, we'd trick our parents and confuse them," said Dino. "If one of us got into trouble, we'd blame it on the other, to get out of the punishment."

"It never worked," said Beni, "they just punished us both!" They laughed in unison.

"It's good to finally meet you, Gilda. Beni's been talking about you for months. Welcome to our home."

Dino and his wife had young children and were eager to prepare for Santa's visit. So after dinner, we excused ourselves and headed out for a cocktail at Scannicchio's.

"Gilda, do you like my family?" Beni asked.

"Of course, what's not to like?" I playfully answered.

"I have to ask you a serious question." He looked at me quite sternly, and I thought he was going to end our relationship.

"What is it?" I said, anticipating the worst.

"I've tried to be honest and open with you about my other family."

"The Mafia?"

"Yes. I need to know if you've come to accept who I am and what I do?" He maintained his serious tone.

"Beni, I accept who you are, but I'm not stupid, I know that your position in the *Family* is more than that of a mere collector," I said.

"Yes it is Gilda... you're very perceptive. I was going to tell you..."

"Now's a good time," I told him, "I'm listening."

"My family has had roots in Sorrento, Italy since the seventeenth century. My grandfather, Don Salvatore Sorrentino, was a respected godfather. He had two sons; my father was the second born. His elder brother took over the running of the *Family* in Italy and my father came here, to America, to build a new territory. He chose Atlantic City, New Jersey. The business was lucrative and our faction prospered. When my father died, my brother and I split the *Family* duties between us. You may not like what we do, but Gilda, I make a good living." Beni paused and awaited my response.

"If you make a good living, why do you need to persecute my parents? They work hard and are good honest people." I needed this answer.

"Gilda, if I made an exception for them, everyone would know and…"

"No, you're wrong. They wouldn't tell a soul. Please Beni?" I begged him.

Beni looked as though he were struggling with a dilemma, so I pushed the point further.

"I've listened carefully to everything you've explained… about your business and your *Family*. I've chosen not to ask questions, nor seek the answers I don't want to hear. I just want one favor, that's all," I pleaded.

"I'd have to seek the agreement of my brother… but Gilda, there's another way to solve this predicament," he said.

"Then please, what is it?"

Again, Beni looked uncomfortable and this time he loosened his tie.

"Gilda, we've been dating these past six months and I believe you've come to care for me," he said.

"Yes, I do care for you Beni and you've always treated me well."

"Gilda, I place you on a pedestal…" Beni paused again and took a deep breath. "Gilda, I love you."

His sudden words of affection prompted his unrestrained hand to dive into his jacket pocket and he pulled out a small gilt box. Then, he knelt down on the floor of the lounge bar.

"Gilda, will you marry me?" he said, offering me a diamond ring.

"Oh Beni! What a beautiful ring! But before I give you my answer, I must have your assurance that you'll stop collecting from my parents." I shamelessly used the moment to get what I needed.

"If you love me Gilda, this is the other way that I can help," he said.

"I do love you Beni, but…"

He placed his index finger against my lips to silence me. "If you accept my proposal, they will automatically become family; we don't collect from spouses' families," he said.

"Then I accept your proposal, but I want it to stop now… *before* we're married." I was insistent.

"Gilda, I'll try, but usually it's after the marriage… damn it Gilda, you drive a hard bargain."

"Then let's get married soon," I said.

Beni looked into my eyes and laughed. "Gilda, you're perfect for me!"

"Ti amo Beni," I reassured him.

"You've made me very happy," he said, exhaling a breath of relief. "Let's go tell the priest."

So we went to midnight Mass as a newly-engaged couple.

*

"Wow, Gilda! A romance with a difference. But I have to ask the million dollar question… did you really fall in love with a Mafioso?" I was skeptical.

"Let's just say that my love was conditional," she answered.

"So, was all this planned?" I asked.

"Ah, I can't fool you Frances! During the six months that I dated Beni, I researched the Mafia in New Jersey. I learnt all about his family and especially about those extended family members who married into the Mafia. They were excluded from the racketeering and the extortion. They were looked after… they had peace of mind."

Gilda sat back with a justified smugness and glowed with satisfaction.

*

On Christmas morning, Neta noticed my ring. It was the elephant in the room.

"Please sit down," I asked Neta and Mendel. "I have something to tell you. I'm getting married."

"No, I forbid it!" Mendel said, leaping to his feet.

"Sit down, Mendel," Neta ordered him. "Gilda knows what she's doing."

"You're right Neta, I do."

I took hold of each of their hands and explained my reasons.

"You took me into your home, you cared for me and I have come to love you both as my own parents. But, I saw an opportunity to start a new life."

"Huh! Cut the crap, Gilda," Neta was surprisingly outspoken. "I know you did it for us."

"I did what's best for *all* of us," I answered.

"What? She's going to marry into the Mafia… no one in their right minds choses that!" said Mendel.

"Mendel, don't be a fool. She did it to release us from the racketeering."

"She can't! I won't allow it!" he protested.

"Gilda, I know I'm right," said Neta.

I nodded.

"Tell me one thing, are you fond of him?" she implored.

"Yes, I am."

"Does he love you?" she asked.

"He does and he treats me well," I assured her.

"But he's Mafia… how can you bear it?" Mendel was distraught.

"I'm a survivor. I'm strong. I'll make it work." I gave him a huge hug.

"I knew all along that you had a plan," said Neta shaking her head. "When is the wedding?"

"We'll marry in January," I said. "Your collections will stop from today."

Neta immediately covered her mouth with her hand to stifle her relief and Mendel shed a tear.

"Not only will you keep all your profits, you'll be looked after for life. There'll be Mafiosi or Associates in the street at all times to protect you," I explained.

"I don't understand," said Mendel. "If the Mafia are no longer collecting, then why would we need protection?" Mendel asked.

"This is good and bad news. Now that you're connected to our Mafia *Family*, other clans and the newly-formed Russian mafia may try to harass you. But, there will be a twenty-four hour Mafia presence to protect both you and the shop," I told them.

"Oh Gilda, what a price you've paid for our peace of mind," Mendel said.

"It's worth it," I said. "You can take a vacation with the extra money, knowing that your shop will be safe. You'll even be able to retire in peace."

"Where will you live Gilda?" Neta asked.

"Beni and his brother have houses on a large compound, just a few miles north of here. The wedding will be held there, too." I said. "Beni will pay for everything and you'll both be my only family in attendance."

"I refuse to go to a Mafioso's home!" said Mendel.

"Then who will give me away?" I said.

"Aye yai yai!" exclaimed Mendel.

"He'll do it," said Neta. "Or he'll have me to deal with!"

"I suppose they're all Catholic?" Mendel said, scowling again.

"Of course. Remember, I was brought up a Catholic, too."

"You'll walk Gilda proudly down the aisle and stand in front of the priest… it's the least you can do, considering her sacrifices for us," Neta told him.

"Why couldn't you find a nice Jewish boy?"

"If she had, we couldn't have afforded the wedding," said Neta. "Count your blessings old man and tell her you'll do it."

"Ah Gilda, I'll proudly walk you down the aisle, I just wish the circumstances were different… but thank you for our peace of mind," he said wiping away another tear and reaching for the bourbon. "Now we'll drink a toast."

*

"Frances, I've had enough emotional recall for today. I need to rest now. For tomorrow, I'll be getting married," she said.

"I look forward to hearing about it," I replied. "It's not every day I get to attend a Mafia wedding."

This was shaping up to be an incredible story of life and death, love and loss and I was eager for the next installment.

The Wedding
Day Seven

"Good morning Gilda. Are you feeling rested?" I said, as I greeted her at breakfast.

"Yes, quite rested, thank you," she said. "Do come and breathe in this air." She was standing by the open French windows and so I joined her.

"I swear this air has cleansed the negative plaque from my soul," she said.

"And was there much to cleanse?" I asked.

"You'll be the judge of that, Frances, when we reach the end of the book. Just be sure not to collect any of your own," she warned.

After breakfast, we settled into our work, accompanied by large cups of freshly-brewed coffee. The aroma awakened our minds and I began recording.

*

The wedding was set for the third Sunday in the month of January. The year was 1971. I was not quite twenty-four years old and I had already encountered more experiences than most people in a lifetime.

Like all young brides-to-be, I'd envisioned a white wedding. But Beni had other ideas.

"Gilda, in southern Italy it was customary for the wedding party to wear black. My grandmother had worn a black wedding dress and all the guests were dressed in black, too. I thought maybe we'd follow the custom," Beni said.

"Black? But I have always dreamed of a white wedding... and the guests will be horrified!" I protested.

"But it's the tradition."

"In Italy, maybe... not here in America," I said. "Did your mother wear black? And what about your brother's wedding...were they all in black, too?" I questioned.

"Well, no they didn't follow the tradition."

"Good, because I've already picked out a white wedding gown and I don't think your brother will want his daughter to be seen in a black bridesmaid's dress."

"My daughter's *not* wearing a black bridesmaid dress!" said Dino, who was within earshot of our conversation. "Are you out of your mind, Beni? My wife will go crazy, besides which, this is 1971... our business associates will think we've just got off the boat!"

Dino turned to me and winked.

"Hey, Roberta!" Dino called his wife. "Beni wants us all to wear black at his wedding, including the bride."

"It's traditional!" Beni tried to protest.

"It's stupid! You're out of your mind! All those guests... powerful business associates, would have to tell their wives to wear black to a contemporary wedding. Gilda, don't listen to him... you're wearing *white*," Roberta said.

Beni could be stubborn, but he was completely outvoted and I was so relieved. But I believe that this tradition still holds in Sicily today.

Neta and I had shopped together for my wedding gown. It had been an emotional process for her as she recalled the sadness of her daughter's death just before her wedding. For me too, it was a time in my life that I'd hoped to enjoy with my mother. We were both casualties of fatal accidents. But we found our conjoining a comfort.

From the time of our engagement, I'd been living with Beni. Security was paramount as I was now an appendage of the Mafia. Their enemies would target me, as a way to hurt Beni. I needed constant protection. At first, it was hard to get used to the lack of privacy; I was shadowed whenever I was outside the compound, but quite free to roam within.

The guest list was long, around three hundred people, most of whom I didn't know. In contrast, my family was comprised of two. Sadly, Eli was too unwell to attend. But I did correspond with him. He said that God had led me to the Mafia so they might help me claim my revenge. An eye for an eye and all that. It had crossed my mind too, but I had plans of my own.

The weather that January was especially cold, so instead of a cavalcade of cars navigating the icy roads to the Catholic church, the priest and the altar were safely transported to the compound, along with the incense, Holy water and six altar boys.

Beni's house had been built to accommodate large groups of people. He entertained frequently, for business and pleasure. The area assigned for our wedding would hold three hundred guests and we'd all stay warm and safe.

The wedding planners were carefully vetted and began assembling the layout the day before the wedding. Gilt chairs for the ceremony were placed in rows in front of the altar, with a red-carpeted aisle between. A reception area was allocated for the bride and groom to receive the guests after the ceremony, with a platform for a band behind them. Tables were set for the wedding breakfast in an adjoining room and marked areas for flower arrangements filled every vacant nook.

Beni slept in a guest room the night before our wedding. But in the morning, he crept back into our bedroom.

"You're not supposed to see me on the morning of the wedding!" I said. "Don't you know it's bad luck?"

"I don't believe that," he said. "Gilda, look at the snow… it's beautiful. What a day we're going to have!" He kissed me. "You're going to make me the happiest man in the world and we'll build a family… have many children."

He was so happy, I couldn't destroy that notion of children. Once again, I secured my secret. Was it deceitful? Probably, but I was taking a huge risk in my life by marrying into the Mafia. And besides, doctors are often wrong.

So, contentedly, we savored our private moment of happiness before the crowd of guests arrived.

*

Things began early, at seven that morning, with the arrival of the caterers. There was enough food to feed an army. The cake was enormous, with four tiers, and the widest I'd ever seen. There was a model of the bride and groom placed on the top. Someone had found a miniature toy model of a gun and placed it under the groom's arm. It was meant as a joke, but I quickly removed it before Mendel and Neta arrived. This was a special day and I didn't want any upsets.

The flowers arrived next, with the bouquets and pins. Everyone was busy. Huge flower arrangements of red and white roses were tethered in place and decorated with ribbons.

At nine in the morning, the band set up on their platform. I remember that the musicians were very temperamental, complaining that their instruments were out of tune due to the cold weather.

A car was sent to collect Neta and Mendel. I wanted my new mother with me, to help me dress. It would be our special moment together.

"Neta, you look beautiful," I said as I greeted my mother and father, as I now called them. "Mendel… Papa!" I teased him. "I've never seen you look so dapper."

"I've never been dressed like a penguin at ten in the morning," he said.

Lastly, the hairstylist and makeup people arrived at ten-thirty to make me look my best. My dress was satin and lace, with white fur trim. I wore a jewel tiara that had belonged to Beni's mother. It clipped onto a full-length veil, part of which came forwards to cover my face.

Dino's daughter was a flower girl, his son a pageboy. Roberta was my matron of honor. His family were now my family, too.

*

Gilda paused.

"Frances, would you like to see some photos?"

"I'd love to," I eagerly answered.

Gilda fetched a faded leather wallet which contained a white wedding album. She opened it and the figure of a beautiful bride leaped from the page.

"That's me, in my wedding dress before the ceremony. Here's my dear mother Neta, arranging my veil."

"You look stunning, Gilda. May I see some more?" I said.

She turned over the page. "This is Beni and me as a married couple," she said.

"He looks very handsome. Just how I'd imagined him, a typical dark haired Italian. You look tiny beside him and so slender and pretty. You make a beautiful couple and your hair… it's so thick and golden."

"Ah yes, my mother's Italian genes are responsible for all that hair. But I inherited the fair color from my father. Now, my hair's a gray, insipid shade and there's less of it. Old age is not attractive."

"Just look at the way Beni's looking at you in this photo, Gilda… he really did love you, didn't he?"

"Yes, I believe he did. You know Frances, there's an old wives' tale, love your husband with all your heart, but love him a little less than he loves you and you will be the happier one."

"If I ever marry again, I'll remember that," I said. "What time was the wedding?"

"It was supposed to be noon, but because it's the custom for Italians — and the guests were mainly Italian — to turn up an hour late, they printed 11:00 a.m. on the invitations," Gilda said.

"And what time did the guests arrive?"

Gilda laughed. "They arrived in droves at precisely 11:45 a.m. ostensibly for the 11:00 a.m. wedding mass, which thankfully began at noon."

*

It was a Nuptial Mass, which I don't think was really allowed outside of a church, but then, as I came to learn, the rules are waived for the Mafia. A Nuptial Mass means that everyone takes Holy Communion, if the bride and groom are both Catholic. Our ceremony took forever, as everyone wanted to be seen taking the sacrament. All the powerful guests, the oil magnates, the business tycoons and the celebrities. The Mafiosi who owned the casinos in Las Vegas and even a couple of senators. All wanted to be noticed.

The capo di tutti (boss) of another Mafia *Family* was invited and they respectfully attended in order to keep the peace. Other clan members were there too, and each came before us in the reception line.

"Beni, there are so many people. How will I remember all their names?" I asked.

"You won't, just smile your beautiful smile. That's enough. Most of them are too scared not to attend and the majority are looking for a favor. This *Family* is just business. Our real family is what matters and you already know all of them."

What he told me was alarming, but true.

However, the Russians were not invited. The Russian mafia had a growing presence in New Jersey, they were increasing in size and competing for racketeering territories. They were ruthless with those who wouldn't, or couldn't, pay.

The Italian Mafia associates were planted everywhere, to guard against confrontations on the streets. I was relieved that I'd found a way to protect Neta and Mendel from these violent predators.

After the speeches, the band began to play the music I'd chosen for my dance with my father. It was an emotional moment for both Mendel and me — he proudly stepped up to the task and we began our dance.

"You are as my own daughter, Gilda. I'm so proud of you. But we are like Ali Baba in a den of thieves... you must be vigilant," he whispered.

"Ah, the story from *The Arabian Nights*. Does that make me the faithful slave-girl who found a way for you to keep your fortune?" I said.

Mendel laughed. "Our secret code, which only we will know, has to be..."

"Open Sesame," I interjected, and we both laughed.

Little did I know that one day that code would become significant in my life.

*

"Gilda, did you ever have second thoughts about the marriage?" I asked.

"About the marriage, or why I did it?" she replied.

"Both," I answered.

"Marrying into the Mafia is not for the faint-hearted. But the man I married was good to me. Do I ever regret the decision? No, never... as you will see in my unfolding story."

*

Beni and I had agreed to postpone our honeymoon for a few months. He had commitments and I wanted to fulfil my obligations to Mendel. They needed me, and I still had commissioned jewelry pieces to complete for several customers, but it was on condition that I find them a replacement. I dreaded that day.

Mafia wives are only supposed to be baby-making machines and history records few exceptions... but even then, I intended to be one of them.

A car was at my disposal at all times, as I was not allowed to walk anywhere alone. All I had to do was click my fingers and the black limousine would ferry me back and forth to the shop three times a week.

But there was one afternoon that I'll never forget.

My driver had arrived early. "Signora Sorrentino, you must return to the compound... it's an emergency," he told me.

"Is it my husband?" I was terrified, as in his business there was always the chance of being shot.

"Signor Beni is fine... it's another *Family* matter. That's all I can say."

When I arrived at the compound I noticed that the guards on the gates had doubled in number. Something was terribly wrong.

"Gilda, thank God you're home," Beni said, wrapping his arms around me.

"What's happened?" I asked, panic-struck.

He ushered me into his office. "Sit down Gilda. The *Family* has been attacked," he said.

Beni sat down beside me and buried his face in his hands. After a minute or two he lifted his head and rubbed his eyes, as if he were disbelieving of the news he was about to convey. "The capo di tutti capi... my uncle, has been murdered."

"Oh! How terrible!"

"There's more," Beni continued. "My uncle was attending a party at a friend's villa in Massa Lubrense, along with his wife and children, when there was a huge explosion. One of the guest's cars had a bomb planted underneath it... God knows how." Beni took out his handkerchief and wiped his eyes. "The villa is usually impregnable... but that's not all."

He took a deep breath in an effort to continue. "The explosion was just a diversion, at that same moment the gates to the property were rammed with a truck and an avalanche of assassins armed with assault weapons... they had HK11s and M10-SMGs..."

My ignorance at the time prevented my knowing exactly what these were. But within a few years, I would become familiar with all the latest weaponry, their capacities and their black-market prices.

Words were difficult, but Beni continued. "They swept up the drive shooting everyone who got between them and their target, my uncle... including my aunt and my young cousins. They're all dead..."

Beni sobbed and I tried to console him, but he was distraught. Then, quite suddenly, he pulled himself up to his full height and walked around the room. It was as if someone had pumped him full of adrenalin.

"The bastards... those fucking lowlife murders. We'll get 'em... all of them," he announced.

The door swung open and Dino came storming into the room, walked right up to Beni, and with arms wide open they consoled each other in a hug. I tactfully turned away so they might share this private moment of grief.

After a few minutes the twin brothers wiped their eyes with their respective white handkerchiefs and sat down to talk.

"You know this alters everything, don't you?" Dino said.

Beni nodded. "I'll make the arrangements. Gilda, we need to prepare," he said.

"Yes of course, I'll pack for the funeral," I said.

"Beni... haven't you told her?" Dino interjected.

"Told me what?" I asked.

"We're going to Italy."

"Of course, I'm going to pack for the..."

"No Gilda, you don't understand. We'll be *living* in Sorrento," he said. "Permanently!"

"Is it definite?" I asked, trying to digest his life changing statement.

"Yes, quite definite. We have no choice," he told me.

I couldn't believe it. We were only just married and now I was emigrating... again. Beni came and sat down beside me.

"Gilda, I want you to listen very carefully to what I'm about say."

He was deadly serious and I was unprepared for more disclosures.

"My uncle, Don Sorrentino, was the godfather of our faction in Campania, the district in which our family lives. But he was also the capo di tutti capi... which means that he was regarded as the supreme head of all the Mafia... the godfather of all godfathers. Do you understand the significance, Gilda?"

I nodded. This information far exceeded that which I'd expected to hear.

"Before a godfather dies, or relinquishes his title, it's traditional for him to choose his successor. His only son, my uncle, was that person — and now he's dead." Beni crossed himself as Catholics do, when they speak of the deceased. "Gilda, what I'm trying to say is that my twin brother Dino and I are his successors. We are the continuation of the bloodline and we are, as of now, the appointed joint godfathers of the Sorrentino *Family*."

My silence was deafening. I couldn't speak. I was in shock. Never in my wildest dreams did I imagine this would happen to me... to us.

"You are now a godfather's wife and will command the respect of our faction and of all southern Italy," he said.

Eventually, I found my voice and asked where in Italy we were to live.

"There are several mansions which sit along the cliffs of Sorrento. My grandfather lives in one of them and we'll live with him," Beni informed me.

"Is it large enough?" I asked.

"Oh yes. It has six luxury suites and an additional five bedrooms in the torre," he said.

"Torre... is the tower?"

"Yes, get used to speaking Italian, Gilda. It'll be our everyday language," he said.

"Don't worry Beni, languages come easily to me. Remember, I have a degree in French, English and German and I also speak Dutch and some

Italian, which I learnt from my mother," I reassured him.

Beni's composure was growing as he steadily dealt with the reality of this life-changing situation.

"Beni, I have a question," I asked. "If your grandfather is still alive, how come *he's* not the godfather?"

"He's too old and frail. When he became bound to a wheelchair, he nominated my uncle as his immediate successor due to his ill-health," Beni explained.

"Will I be expected to care for him?" I asked.

"Oh no, he has a team of special nurses who care for him around the clock. But I think he will delight in your beautiful presence," Beni said, and leaned forward to kiss me.

"You'll love Sorrento, with its beautiful views of the bay and the isle of Capri. Oh, and the lemons!" In a gesture of love, he pinched his index finger and thumb together against his lips in a kiss. "Our family has many hectares of lemon groves."

Beni was mentally embracing our new home, but I still had questions. "How will we stay safe in Sorrento after these murders?" I asked. "Won't the same people come after us, too?" I was frightened.

"We intend to overhaul the security. Know this Gilda, I would never let anything happen to you. I will guard you with my life," he told me.

I think this is when I truly registered the grave danger of my daily existence. We were going to bury four members of his family and six loyal men of honor who'd served the Sorrentino faction for two decades. They were the best, but even they could not have stopped this massacre. I was afraid, but for Beni's sake, I tried not to show it.

*

"Frances, I need to stop for the day, I have an appointment," Gilda said, checking the clock.

"Of course Gilda, we've had an eventful day," I said.

She looked somewhat perturbed as she hurried out of the room. She didn't volunteer information about her destination, neither did I ask. My role was as transcriber of her memoirs, without intrusion into her present. I respected her right to privacy.

Italy

Day Eight

"Good morning, Frances," Gilda said, handing me a cup of coffee.

Her hand was shaking slightly, so I quickly grasped the cup. "Thank you, and good morning to you too," I said.

"Are you ready to accompany me to Italy?" she said.

"Ready when you are," I agreed, noting that she looked unusually tired this morning.

"Recording day eight…"

*

I sat with Neta and Mendel and relayed the tragedy. They were shocked and concerned for my safety. "Will you accompany Beni to Italy for the funeral?" Neta had asked.

I tried to break this news gently, but there was no easy way to explain it. I paused and let my gaze rest on them each in turn.

"What is it?" Mendel said.

"Beni and Dino… they are the joint successors of the faction…"

"Oh no!" Neta's hand covered her mouth.

"When do you leave?" said Mendel.

"This week. Actually, I have three days to pack," I said.

Tears streamed down my face as I lunged forward to hug my parents. Neta cried, too. I remember the moisture of our salty tears as they mingled on our cheeks and fell onto Neta's white napkins, that we snatched from the table, already set for dinner. Leaving them was another sadness I would have to endure.

"Perhaps you could talk to Beni… get him to change his mind and stay?" Mendel had asked.

Then, Neta naively asked, "Could you persuade him to leave the Mafia?"

"When I first began dating Beni I thought I could change him… persuade him to leave the Mafia. But I quickly became educated in their way of life and had to accept the fact that if I married Beni, I would also be married to the Mafia," I explained.

"Your sacrifice for our peaceful life has amounted to more than we had imagined. We won't pressure you again, dear Gilda," said Neta.

I held onto each of their hands as I spoke. "You both know that I made a deal of my own free will. I'm married now and I have to go with my husband. The only consolation is that you will be safe."

*

"You see Frances, no one leaves the Mafia… unless they're in a coffin," Gilda said.

"I did," I said.

"Yes, you're a brave woman. You had the courage to invent a story and make false promises to facilitate your escape."

"And you were my salvation, for which I'm truly grateful," I said.

Gilda smiled and gently touched my hand.

"I'm pleased you're here… but remember, Frances, you weren't married to a Mafioso and your ex-partner only became a *made man* after you left. I married a Mafioso who was ranked highly within the faction; and then the unthinkable happened and I became the wife of the godfather! Can you imagine that?" she said.

"So even if you'd considered leaving the marriage…"

"A deal was sanctioned. I had sold my soul to protect my new parents. You have to realize that although I was newly married, I already knew too much about the *Family*. I could never leave," Gilda said.

"But eventually you *did* leave."

"No. In my position as the godfather's widow, I'm still officially part of the Sorrentino faction. I can never truly sever my ties… I know too many secrets."

"Am I to learn these secrets too?" I asked.

"Yes, Frances. But you're just the messenger, so to speak."

"And will they shoot the messenger?"

"Only if they read the manuscript before publication. Don't worry, once we publish the whole world will learn these secrets," she said.

"But Gilda, we both know that Dino will seek retribution."

"Yes, that is the way of the Mafia. It'll be me he comes after, not you, my dear. I intend to write a clause exonerating you from all blame, as I'm the one with the inside knowledge."

"But Gilda, aren't you afraid of being harmed?"

"I'm getting older… I'm running out of time, Frances. There's nothing they can do," she said, smiling gently.

Was she trying to tell me something other than the obvious? My suspicions were aroused, but I said nothing and let the moment pass.

"Secrets and lies can only prevail in silence. The best method for exposing abuse, in all its forms, is to break that silence and you and I are about to shout about it," Gilda said. "But not on an empty stomach. Let's have lunch."

*

I was the perfect Mafia bride. Keeping secrets was easy for me. I grew up with parents who'd taken on false identities to survive the second world war. I knew how to keep family secrets.

It was less than ten years since I'd emigrated to America and now I would be returning to Europe. But this time, to a country that had allied itself with Germany.

I put aside my sadness with the understanding that I would return to visit my parents two or three times a year. This new phase of my life was packed with as many advantages as disadvantages, and I was resigned to acting in a positive manner.

*

A professional company affiliated to the Mafia packed up our home and all our personal belongings in a couple of days. We flew with only a couple of suitcases —the remainder was shipped.

"Hold my hand, Gilda," Beni had requested at the airport. "I want to mark this special occasion… it's the beginning of our new life together."

"We're *returning* to Italy Beni, remember. I'm half Italian. This will be a genetic homecoming for me," I said, feeling excited. "Italy is in my blood."

Our flight to Naples was accompanied by members of our immediate faction: two soldiers, also known as made men, and one capo — a higher-ranking Mafioso — who sat with us in first class. Dino and his family had flown the day before, to prevent the two godfathers from traveling together… just in case of a mishap.

We were met at Naples airport by members of the *Family*, who had organized a convoy of three black sedans. We traveled between the two outer cars, for security reasons. Our daily life would be more protected as the risk of attack would be higher. For now, we were a universal target.

The drive from Naples was only twenty-six miles. Beni knew the route well and as we approached the coast of Sorrento, he became excited, like a child nearing their vacation destination.

"Look Gilda, up there," Beni said, pointing to the white mansion perched on the edge of the cliff.

Although it was winter, the watery sun light threw a nacreous effect upon the exterior of the house, sitting as a pearl within an oyster-shaped bay. It was love at first sight, and I understood why artists flocked to this coast to capture on canvas these whimsical impressions.

A housekeeper, clothed in black mourning garments, greeted us at the door as the security carried out a sweep of the area. We were ushered directly into one of the large living rooms where Beni's grandfather was seated. He had once been a strong man, feared by many, but his body had withered into fragility and he was confined to a wheelchair. Beni bent down to kiss his grandfather and respectfully introduced me.

I remember that his bony hand griped mine tighter than I'd expected, and it pulled me close towards him. He looked into my eyes as if he were searching for something or somebody. Then he said in Italian that I reminded him of his wife. This pleased Beni immensely. He made the sign of the cross and mumbled that the saints had blessed us and this turn of events was meant to be.

"Our living quarters will be on the east side of the mansion," Beni informed me. "Cara mia, we'll see the sunrise from our bed…oh it's so good to be back in Sorrento." In spite of all the horrors and sadness, there was happiness in his voice.

"The beauty of this place will wipe away our tears," I told him.

"I feel this is a fresh beginning for us Gilda. We'll make our babies here in our new home," he said.

Every godfather dreams of having a son to succeed them. And, maybe that doctor in Minneapolis made the wrong diagnosis. It's happened before.

The Mafia families are devout Catholics. I feared Beni would not have married me, had I divulged my secret about Gary's birth or adoption. So I never told him I'd given birth to a son. I just kept reminding myself how imperative the marriage deal had been for the safety of my dear parents.

Secrets and lies kept me safe within the Mafia. It was my survival technique.

*

Two days before the funerals, the six family coffins, containing Beni's uncle, his wife and their four children, were laid out in a reception hall. Although it was customary to have open caskets, after the bomb the bodies had been unrecognizably dismembered and too horrific to display.

The Italians follow strict traditions, especially for funerals. Friends and family members brought food and wine as gifts to the house for us during our time of mourning. The Italians believe this to be a time of reflection, not cooking. They were immensely generous.

The family funerals were to be held on the Friday following our arrival. Beni, his grandfather and I were the first of the cavalcade to arrive at the church.

"Beni, look at all the people!" The church was full and the crowds were overflowing down the steps.

Beni and Dino were two of the pallbearers for his uncle. "Gilda, what if I drop the coffin? What if..."

"You'll be okay. Ti amo."

Beni sniffed loudly. "Do I have a handkerchief, Gilda?" he asked.

"Yes, of course," I said and gently pulled one from his pocket. "It's quite normal to feel nervous when you're upset," I said. I straightened his tie and kissed him and he alighted, reassured.

It would have shocked the faction to see that their godfather had a vulnerable side. They'd have viewed it as weakness and taken advantage of him. But that was the private side of Beni, and the part I loved.

When the deceased are lying in their caskets it's the custom for family to kiss their cheeks or foreheads. It's a symbolic gesture and shows respect. But because the coffins were closed, the mourners came forward and kissed the coffins instead, and so did we.

The Mass was long and so very sad. The sight of the children's white coffins was particularly hard to bear. I turned my eyes upward and wondered for that split second whether my accident had been a blessing in disguise. I would never have Mafia-born children, and I would never have to bury them.

But God was playing me. Years later my son Gary would be killed... ironically, by the Mafia.

The actual graveside burials were attended only by close family. Each one of the men threw a fist full of dirt on the lowered caskets and the women threw flowers. The family plot was large and, afterwards, Beni walked me to his plot.

"Gilda, I want to introduce you to my parents… may they rest in peace," he said and crossed himself. "They would have loved you, as I do," he said, squeezing my hand.

"I'm sure I'd have loved them too," I said.

"Today has been a trial. I don't know how I'd have coped without you."

"Do you believe they're all with God now?" I asked him.

"Yes, I do. I try not to rationalize my religion and just accept that it's all about faith and forgiveness. In Italy, tradition and religion are synonymous. It's our way of life," he said. "But one thing I do know… God sent you to love and comfort me."

I felt valued and protected by this man, despite his way of life. If I'd had a dime with the word 'love' on one side and 'death' on the other, I'd have spun it daily. Whichever way it landed dictated the order of business. Nothing was predictable except Omerta… and this was Beni's creed.

Italian Life
Day Nine

"Frances, do you like the opera?" Gilda asked.

"I love it," I answered.

"Then you'll have heard the name… Caruso," Gilda said.

*

After the solemn funerals I welcomed an initiation celebration to be held on the Sunday.

The restaurant, Ristorante Museo Caruso, in Sorrento, was the family's favorite place to eat. This famous restaurant pays homage to the legendary opera singer, Caruso… a favorite of Beni's grandfather. It was a family occasion and the place was sequestered, swept by security and surrounded by a Mafia guard.

The restaurant's walls were covered with photographs of Caruso from his performances at various venues around the world. Displayed on a prominent table was an old fashioned gramophone which played Caruso's music continuously, day and evening. The dining areas were relatively small, but tables were assembled together so as to accommodate the prodigious family members.

The lunch was served in five courses. I had never in my life tasted food that good. Each dish was perfect. The wine flowed all day and in between the dessert and cheeses came the toasts.

Beni's grandfather spoke first. "We are used to tragedy in our family. Sadly, this assassination was personal… but we will make it our business to retaliate. It is a question of honor. I welcome my grandsons, Dino and Beni as the joint successors to our faction." He raised his glass in a toast. "Ai padrini!"

"I padrini!" we all said in unison.

"Thank you Nonno," said Dino. "My brother and I are honored to command this faction. We will serve you, Nonno, and my deceased uncle with honor."

Everyone clapped and then Beni stood.

"God bless you Nonno, and thank you for welcoming us back to

Sorrento," Beni said, blowing his grandfather a kiss. "Our family has had roots in this region since the seventeenth century. It feels good to come home." I clapped with the rest of them.

"My uncle was a fair and powerful godfather whom my brother and I will strive to emulate. Our vendetta continues beyond his death and the murder of his family… may they rest in peace." And he made the sign of the cross.

"May they rest in peace," everyone repeated, also making the sign of the cross.

"They will be avenged!" Beni shouted. There were cheers in the room. Beni raised his glass and said loudly…"Omerta!"

Everyone stood…"Omerta," the whole room replied, and then they clapped.

It wasn't until that moment, when I looked around at the faces of the Mafiosi who had pledged their loyalty to my husband, that I truly realized the power Beni commanded.

Music began again and the celebrations continued.

"Beni, you spoke as a true leader," I told him. "I'm so proud of you."

"The blood of my ancestors runs in my veins. It's a powerful feeling, Gilda. This is my destiny. We will thrive in Italy," he told me.

"And what will my purpose be?" I asked.

"You will do what every Mafia wife does, Gilda… make babies," he said.

*

During that first month, there was much Mafia business to sort out. Beni and Dino shared the leadership duties of the faction and made joint decisions concerning the businesses. They allocated the less significant decisions to Piero, the consigliere, who'd been their uncle's right hand man for many years. Next in line was the capo. There would be two Mafiosi sharing this position; Frankie — who'd traveled with us — and Marco, who knew the Italian ways. They were in charge of the soldiers… the made men. Then, there were the Italian associates. They were essential for ongoing business ventures and would take a share of any profits in which they cut a deal. But they were the most vulnerable area of security, as they were prone to leaking information or double dealing. All Mafiosi, except the associates, took the oath of silence, the Omerta; pledging trust and willingness to die for the *Family*. Some associates would prove their loyalty and eventually become made men.

*

"Gilda, I vaguely remember that to become a made man, you have to be called by the godfather, is that correct?"

"Yes Frances, and sometimes the godfather's call was not what they were expecting," she replied. "But of course your ex-partner, Tom, was about to become a made man by Dino, when you left Italy."

"How strange these connections between us Gilda," I said, wondering what else I'd discover. We paused our work for an appropriate Italian lunch…a shared antipasto platter.

*

"I'd like to skip forward a few months to the summer of 1971… my first experience of the glorious Italian weather," Gilda said.

I switched on my voice recorder and Gilda began.

*

I remember the impact of my first summer in southern Italy. Tables with colorful umbrellas occupied the sidewalks and filled the town square. Daily life would be lived outside for the next part of the year. The aromas of flowers and food filled the air and the population of Sorrento exploded with tourists. These families would dine early, unlike the Italian locals, who would sit for an hour or two after work sipping wine or vermouth cocktails and nibbling on plates of antipasti. Then, around 9:30 or 10 p.m. they'd either go home for a family dinner or head to their favorite restaurants.

It took me a while to get used to this schedule of rising early and dining late. I think that's why the Latins invented the necessary siesta. Needless to say, I had fallen in love with Italy and quickly adjusted.

I'd taken to spending time with Nonno. I would visit him almost every day around 5 p.m. when he would take a glass of limoncello.

"When Nonna and I were first married," he told me, "she would try out various recipes for limoncello. We'd sit together at 5 p.m., just like us Gilda, and taste the fresh batch. I'd give her my opinion and we'd rate the different recipes, scoring them out of ten."

"Did Nonna invent the limoncello recipes?" I asked.

"Yes, some. But others had been passed down through her family for generations," Nonno explained.

"Do you still have her recipes?" I enquired.

"I do. Wheel me into the bedroom," he instructed.

71

I steered him to a bureau, where he retrieved a large painted box.

"This belonged to Nonna," he said, as he opened the lid and lifted a bundle of letters tied in a red ribbon. "These are the letters I sent her during our times apart."

"How long were you married?" I asked.

"Fifty years and all of them filled with love. I miss her every day." His eyes filled with tears as he spoke of his past love.

I squeezed his hand to signal that I understood. "My parents had a loving marriage too," I said.

"Here they are." He pulled out a buff colored envelope, tarnished with time. Inside were a dozen limoncello recipes. "I want you to have these," he said.

"Thank you Nonno, I'm honored," I told him.

I read them thoroughly that night and approached Nonno the next day with my idea.

"I'd like to make batches of each recipe for you to try," I told him.

"Meraviglioso! And you and I will continue the family tasting tradition together," he said, smiling with delight.

I studied Nonna's notes and learned the tradition of the Campania district:

LEMONS: The most important difference in the quality of limoncello is the lemons. Sorrento lemons are sweet. The cultivation system depends on the microclimate and proximity to the sea. The locally grown lemons are harvested between February and October and must be protected from cold winds by traditional straw matting, referred to as... pagliarelle. These mats are laid on the ground to cover the groves and held up with three-and-a-half metres of chestnut poles. The lemons are carefully picked by hand and must never be dropped. It's important to know the origin of the citrus fruit as the taste depends on the varieties within the region. Femminiello, from Massa Lubrense is a smooth skinned oval lemon and very juicy. Sfusato, from Amalfi, is a larger, thicker skinned, tapered lemon, with few seeds. Both these types influence the intense aroma, produced by the essential oils that they inherit from the environment.

Recipe:

INGREDIENTS: Sorrento lemons, alcohol, sugar.

10 lemons

One bottle (750 ml) of grain alcohol, vodka or grappa.

Four cups water (filtered tap or distilled water)

Three cups of sugar
Multiply x times.
METHOD: Wash the lemons in warm water, using a brush to remove any residue of insecticides. Use only high quality alcohol, this prevents the liqueur from turning to ice in the freezer. Pour the alcohol into a jug with pieces of the rind. Cover and keep in a dark room for one month at room temperature. The instilled liquid slowly assumes the aroma and the yellow tones from the lemons. After one month, add a boiled and cooled jug of water and sugar and more grappa or vodka. Keep as before for a further month. After approximately forty days, filter the instilled liquid and discard the peels. Pour into bottles and place in the ice house. - Nowadays it would be the freezer. - No artificial coloring or additives are added to the liquor.

Recipe for crèma di limoncello: make with milk instead of sugar.

Once the first batch was placed in the dark for thirty days, I began the next. I repeated this procedure through four of Nonna's differing recipes.

After two months, the first batch was ready for tasting. I proudly took the chilled bottle with two glasses on a tray to Nonno.

"Tell me the truth Nonno, is it good or not?" I asked.

He began by swirling the limoncello around in the glass. "It's a good color," he said. Next he lifted the glass to his nose and inhaled the aroma. "The oils have been well absorbed," he noted. Then he took his first sip of the yellow nectar and savored it in his mouth before he swallowed.

"Well?" I said, impatiently.

"Patience, Gilda. This is Italy, not America."

I was put firmly in my place.

"It's not too acidic and not too sweet. It has perfect balance," he said. Then he looked me squarely in the face and said, "It's as if Nonna had made it herself." And he raised his glass to me. "Perfetto!"

This was the best compliment.

We repeated this ritual through all the recipes, as Nonno analyzed each blend and graded them out of ten. "We all have varying palates," he said. "Variety is good, but in my old age, my preference is for something sweet."

*

I had not conceived by August and Beni was disappointed. I was not surprised and assumed the doctor's diagnosis had been correct, although

I had hoped for a miracle and prayed hard for a son.

I was not the type of woman to sit around knitting and gossiping. I needed to use my brain. I also had a plan. Without conforming to motherhood, I would make myself indispensable… yet another survival technique.

"Beni, while we're waiting for God to bless us with children, I would like to talk with you about a business proposition," I said.

"I'm always open to your ideas, Gilda." he confirmed and he was a good listener.

I chose a time for an undisturbed presentation and then I laid out a tray with four glasses of limoncello.

"What are we celebrating?" he'd asked, looking at the display.

"A new family business," I told him. "Please, taste each glass of limoncello and give me your opinion."

Beni relished each sip of my homemade limoncello, lavishing me with rapturous compliments after each taste. He rated each, but almost all were a ten.

"I've used Nonna's recipes, which Nonno has kept all these years," I explained. "As we have extensive lemon groves, I want to start a business… it will be our special brand of limoncello. Here's my business plan," I said, handing him a sheet in which I'd laid out my start-up costs and profit forecast.

Beni took a few minutes to read it. "Gilda, this is spectacular. I'll pass it by Dino, but I'm sure he'll be in favor."

"Why not arrange a time for drinks with all our family, and surprise them with a tasting?" I suggested.

Beni agreed.

The following day I set up the terrace for the gathering. I set out the glasses and kept the several varieties of limoncello on ice. Then, I collected Nonno and wheeled him into pride of place.

Once everyone was present, I announced the tasting of "Nonna's limoncello".

Everyone assembled enjoyed the variety and the vote was unanimous and my idea, that we produce limoncello from our own lemons, was sanctioned.

"What will you call it?" asked Dino.

I glanced at Nonno. "Nonna's limoncello, of course," I said. They all applauded and Nonno blew me a kiss.

Beni and I set up the venue for the processing and production. Staff were hired and contracts established. Two weeks later, we were in the liqueur business. We had two-and-a-half months to prepare as much as we could before the lemon harvest ended.

The business was a huge success and we roared into the new year with a bumper lemon harvest due in the February of 1972.

By that summer, I had proved myself to be more than a baby making machine — and I was only twenty-five.

*

"Frances... ironically it's 5 p.m. Shall we have a drink?" Gilda proposed.

"Do you have anything special in mind?" I asked, grinning widely.

"Take a wild guess," she said, and laughed.

A Mafia Wife
Day Ten

"Good morning Frances!" Gilda greeted me as usual with her beautiful smile.

"Good morning," I replied. "I can't believe we're on day ten."

"Ready to hear more about my Mafia career?" she said.

"Can't wait," I said and switched on my voice recorder and Gilda began.

*

By the fall of 1972 I'd been in business a year and we were already expanding our production premises. Although Beni was proud of my achievement, he was still hopeful I'd discover motherhood. I knew it to be unlikely, so I threw myself into yet another venture.

The Sorrentino family not only owned much land with lemon groves, they owned olive groves too. So I proposed an olive oil business. I followed up my proposal with a business plan and on the strength of my success with the limoncello, I won the confidence of the family. Production began with the first harvest that fall.

It was undeniable that I had a talent for business. My parents had instilled in me a work ethic which I applied to all areas of my life. I had acquired management skills, creative accounting and common sense. I truly believe that good business judgement comes from experience, whatever the business. So, I applied my talent to olive oil with much success.

The two business ventures worked well together. Harvesting olives in the fall and through the winter and harvesting lemons through the spring and summer. Previously, the olives had been sold raw, but I had generated a modern business using the Sinolea method, which was a new technological invention for extracting the oil from olives. In time, we added a lemon-flavored oil to our production too, which made good use of our stock of inferior lemons.

I was having fun and I wanted to keep our business clean and unconnected with Mafia corruption. But after a year, I discovered a serious problem affecting the business, so I spoke to Beni.

"Beni, the other Families in Italy are corrupting the olive oil business," I'd explained. "They're buying bad grade oil, relabeling it and exporting it as high grade virgin oil. They're giving the industry a bad name. Special tasting experts are opening the exports randomly and those brands are being banned from sale," I told him.

"How does that affect *us*?" he asked.

"I've heard from a reliable source that our Sorrentino brand is being interrupted on its export journey. Our good virgin oil is being stolen and replaced with low grade. Our Sorrentino family brand is sold as counterfeit," I explained. "The clans are forging our brand label... Sorrentino Virgin Olive Oil and pasting our labels on bottles containing low grade oil, which makes us vulnerable to the customs and excise agencies, who will pursue us for fraud and seize our goods."

"How will they know?" asked Beni.

"They employ expert tasters, who can detect the slightest difference in the grade of oil. If we're caught by the tasters it will finish our business and ruin our brand," I explained.

"You've a good business head... I'll sort it," Beni agreed. "And it seems that you're well connected. Who's your source?"

"Sure, Beni. But before I tell you, I want your word that he'll stay safe... I need him to feed me information about rival businesses," I said.

"Alright, you have my word, but we'll do the culling *my* way."

I thanked him and as I turned to leave, he caught my arm and pulled me close.

"You're good for our family Gilda... you're one of us now." he said and kissed me passionately. "Your business sense excites me. Lock the door, I want you now... here."

*

"Oh how I remember his passion! Even though I'm old, these memories still make me tingle," Gilda said.

"I can tell," I replied. "Gilda, you're glowing."

"The marriage was good at first, before the subject of *babies* became an ongoing issue," she said, wandering off into a mental haze. After a few minutes I called her name and she re-engaged.

"Yes, Frances, the moment has passed — and now it's time to let the memories settle back into an undisturbed past." And so she continued.

*

The Mafia had their own ways of dealing with anyone who crossed them in business and it wasn't pretty. They literally wiped the opposition out. I found the violence repugnant, and of course the racketeering corruption was the reason I'd made the deal for my parents. It was a wilful decision, I wasn't forced into marriage and Beni was a good husband to me. Often, I had to pinch myself… here I was, living in one of the famous mansions of Sorrento, married to the godfather of the most prestigious faction in southern Italy. It was surreal!

There was plenty of money, which was gained illicitly, except for that earned by my businesses. But there was also time for fun. We'd fly up to Milan for the fashion season. I'd attend the runway shows while Beni conducted business. We traveled often to Florence, Rome and Venice, where we'd visit with old family friends. But best of all, every few months I'd travel back to the States to spend time with my dear parents. Wherever we went, together or alone, we were chaperoned for our own safety by the soldati. We were constantly vigilant and aware that any day there could be a kidnapping or a bullet with our name on it. These good times came at a price.

As a godfather's wife, I was trusted. I was also a proven business woman. Beni and Dino had a huge business income. The list of criminal activities included labor racketeering in Naples and Sorrento, except for Caruso's restaurant… *that* was sacrosanct. They were into gambling, extortion, arson, loan sharking, tax evasion, pornography, counterfeiting and narcotics. I asked him not to deal in drugs, but I was told it was not my concern.

My businesses grew exponentially, but I needed more to occupy my mind. So I placed my limoncello and olive oil businesses in the hands of trusted Mafia managers. I used my head, and set about learning the business of finance and evolving technology. It was a decade before computer usage became commonplace; eventually I would become computer literate and develop a database for our faction. But this was the time before the tech explosion, and I used it efficiently. I learnt everything I could about all our Mafia business dealings. I studied all the files, kept notes on everyone we dealt with and listened to all the business meetings until I knew enough to approach Beni once again about a work idea.

"Beni, it's 1975… I'm twenty-eight and sadly, we have no bambini. I need to work to keep sane. I've identified some ways in which your business is run inefficiently. I think I can improve things, if you give me a chance to work with you."

"Gilda, you're a woman! No women have access to Mafia business… it's unheard of," he told me.

I immediately placed a document in front of him, outlining all the improvements that I could implement. "Please read," I said and walked away to give him space.

About half an hour later, he called me back.

"Okay, I've read this," he said, waving the document at me, "and it's good. You always were clever Gilda, but how do I explain having a woman—"

"I'm the godfather's wife and you know I'm trusted and well respected. Haven't I proved it, by founding two businesses?" I said, quite confidently.

"There's no doubt that you're clever and would be an asset, but Gilda… you're asking too much."

"You're the most powerful man in southern Italy. Why not take a stand and make a statement? I *want* to work," I said. "Please Beni, I need this."

Beni sat and twirled in his chair. Then he called Dino to the office.

"Gilda wants to work inside the business with us," he told him. "Do you object?"

Dino was stunned. He glanced at me and then back to Beni.

"Are you *mad*? A woman involved in our business?"

"Excuse me," I said, "I am here, you know."

"Gilda, it's not personal, but you don't know how things work."

"Yes, she does," interrupted Beni, "take a look at this." And he passed Dino the document I'd compiled.

Dino sat and read my proposal. After ten minutes of digesting it, he shared his opinion. "You know Beni, these suggestions would be good for us. We'd make more dough and our operations would run more efficiently. At the moment it's chaos," he said.

"Yeah, I know, it's just that no other boss has a woman in their business. We'd be a laughing stock," Beni said.

"Actually, there have been several Mafia queens," I told them. "They usually take over the running of their late husband's faction."

Beni scratched his head. "What would Nonno say? I need his opinion. Gilda please wheel him in," Beni asked, "and *don't* tell him what it's about."

I dutifully fetched Nonno and he sat, bemused, in the middle of the room. Beni and Dino explained my proposal.

"So what do you think, Nonno? Should we include a woman? Would the other clans disrespect us?" Dino said.

"A woman? This is *Gilda* we're talking about! She's no ordinary woman. She's smarter than the both of you and she's gained the respect of our family and the clans," Nonno said emphatically. "She's the best thing that's happened to our family and unlike some of your soldiers, I'd trust her with my life."

Nonno turned and blew Gilda a kiss. "That's quite an endorsement," Dino said.

"So you think we should include her."

"Of course," he said. "Are you imbeciles? Didn't you hear me? Of *course* you should include her. She's proven that she has a fine head for business."

He was quite adamant and the twin godfathers were blown away by his statement.

I walked over to his chair, "Caro mio, grazie," I said and bent down and kissed him.

"Gilda is a true Mafia queen," said Nonno, raising both his arms to his grandsons in a grand gesture.

"So it's settled," said Beni. "Fetch a bottle of limoncello."

And so we drank to my induction into the financial side of our Mafia business.

*

"Frances, it's time for lunch," Gilda said, and I agreed.

*

I set to work immediately. My goal was efficiency. I managed to control and cull the payments that were bleeding our finances. I made the soldiers account for the hours they worked, so they'd be paid accordingly. I handled bonuses and special paid jobs, and ran our operation like a professional CFO. I supervised all the deals, managed the debts, the friends… and the enemies.

After I'd reorganized the Italian *Family,* I turned my attention to our New Jersey faction. When we left Atlantic City, Beni and Dino had promoted a trusted consigliere to the position of boss. He would run the NJ faction on behalf of the godfathers. My next task was to visit the NJ boss and check out the books. If he was scamming us, I'd find discrepancies.

"Gilda, I want our visit to the NJ office to be a surprise," Beni had said. "We'll tell no one… agreed?"

"Agreed," I'd replied.

"This is the plan. I'll take Tony out to eat and leave you in the office with access to the accounts. They've got one of those new photocopy machines, so copy anything that looks suspicious."

"Of course Beni, I know the drill," I said.

"Yeah, I don't need to tell you anything, do I? You're the Mafia queen," and he laughed.

My greatest thrill in travelling back to the States was to visit with my parents, but I was not allowed to warn them of our plans, either.

*

We landed early in the morning at Newark airport in New Jersey. Private cars had been arranged by our Italian security, who flew with us. We weren't taking any chances. Our car drew up outside the jewelry shop, just as Mendel was unlocking the door.

"He looks worried Beni," I said. "I can tell that he thinks we're the other Mafia."

I rolled down the window and called to him, "Papa," was all I said.

At first he was startled. "Mendel, it's me, Gilda," I called again.

His face transformed into an emotional smile, "Gilda!" he said. "How—""

I ran and threw my arms around him and we stood there in the street, hugging.

"You see Mendel, I'm a man of my word. I promised she'd visit and here she is," Beni said, smiling.

Words failed Mendel. He just grabbed Beni's hand in appreciation. "Let's find Neta," he said. "But I warn you, she hates surprises!" he said with a wicked grin.

I walked into the kitchen, where Neta was clearing up. She turned around to scold Mendel and jumped.

"Oh my God! You trying to give me a heart attack? Where did you come from? Why didn't you tell us?"

"Too many questions," said Mendel. "Just be happy we have her back with us… at least for a while."

I hugged Neta and we both cried. I'd missed them so much.

"Where's Beni?" she said.

"He's making a surprise call on the *Family*," I said. "That's why we couldn't give you advance notice."

"Mendel, close the shop, we need to sit and talk… be a family again," Neta said.

So we spent the next two hours talking. We reminisced about our time together and I told them all about Italy.

"I've personally founded two businesses," I said, explaining about the limoncello and the olives. "Based on my success, I proposed that I get involved in overhauling the financial side of our *Family* business and making it more efficient. Now, I'm officially part of Italian operations. I effectively manage the finances of the Sorrentino *Family* and Beni wants me to check the NJ faction, too."

They looked concerned.

"I needed something to do," I said. "You both know that it's unlikely I'll have children, although I had hoped that diagnosis was wrong."

I'd kept no secrets from them, so they knew why there were no babies. "Has Beni guessed your secret?" Neta asked.

"No, and I can never tell him. In Italy, if you're not blessed with bambini, the family accept that it's God's will," I told them. "I'm working to make myself indispensable in other ways… it's my survival plan."

"Is it so hard to survive?" Mendel asked.

"No, but I'm always vigilant," I said. "As the *Family* come to rely on me I'll gain power and liberty. Then I can travel and spend more time with you both."

"You're a clever girl to devise such a plan," Mendel said.

Later that day, Beni sent a car to transport me to the office. "I have to work now, but I'll return tomorrow and we'll have lots of time together," I said as I kissed their happy faces goodbye.

*

The NJ boss, Tony, was surprised that I'd be checking the books. Firstly, because I was a woman and secondly, because he wasn't expecting it. I remember the look of contempt he gave me precisely because I was a woman — he obviously didn't expect me to be an efficient accountant, either. He was in for a surprise!

Beni took him out to eat and left me well guarded. I had approximately two hours in which to find anything irregular.

I worked diligently through the books and noted the unusual payments. It was laborious work, but I had developed a keen eye for detail and a nose for fraud. After half an hour of sniffing around, I was alerted to some invoices which didn't tally. In these cases there is always an alternative ledger and I found it, hidden away in an unlocked safe. The recorded payments were quite different from the main accounting books. It was evident that *this* ledger was never meant for our eyes. I also found a grocery bag at the back of the safe containing wads of cash bound in $100 bundles. Also unaccounted for, I presumed.

In Tony's desk drawer there was another bag, with rolled bundles of bills held in purple rubber bands that had been removed from broccoli. I laughed, as this was a trademark of the Mafia. If you took out your roll of money at a vendor's shop, the purple band would signal you were Mafia and God help anyone who didn't comply with your demands.

I took the ledger and the cash and also the allegedly legitimate accounting books. It seemed likely that Boney Tony would have some explaining to do. Beni would not be pleased.

On his return from lunch, Beni drew me aside. "Well Gilda? Did you find anything?"

"I have all I need," I said, discreetly showing him my case with the accounting ledgers and more.

"Tony, we're going to borrow a few items," Beni told him. "Ciao." And we left the office.

Back in our hotel room, I laid out my discoveries and explained the financial discrepancies to Beni. He was smart, but not a financial genius, so he listened carefully.

"He's running a scam, Beni," I said and showed him the dual accounting ledgers.

"I'll kill him," said Beni, reading the amounts.

"That's not all," I said, and produced the cash.

"I'll fucking kill him… he's a dead man walking!"

"Before you kill him, we could trap him," I suggested.

Beni listened carefully as I explained how.

The following day, we entered the NJ office as if nothing had been discovered. Beni greeted Tony like an old friend and kept him talking while I slipped into the back room, ostensibly to return the books.

Tony was apprehensive. "Everything okay, boss?" he asked.

"Sure Tony, why d'ya ask?" Beni replied.

"I wondered why you had a woman — sorry boss, your wife — look at the books."

"You know how women are. Gives her something to do," Beni said.

"Yeah and she's a looker... you don't want the guys hanging around her." Tony paused, cleared his throat and continued. "Thought she might be one of those career girls, you know, book keeping or such?"

Tony was fishing.

"Who, Gilda? Nah, she wants bambinos... God willing, many bambinos," Beni said and laughed.

Tony's expression lightened and he slapped Beni on the back in a manly gesture. "You have work to do my friend!" and he too laughed.

While they were busy talking, I placed a bug under Tony's desk and unscrewed the telephone receiver, where I carefully placed another. I'd kept copies of all that I needed and so I returned the books to their original place and joined Beni.

We smiled and joked some more and left Tony alone.

"Did you fix things, Gilda?" Beni asked.

"Of course," I replied.

"Now, we wait and listen," said Beni, having switched to a serious mood.

*

It didn't take long before Tony was on his phone, boasting to his cronies about how stupid Beni was to have a *broad* check his books. Better still, he arranged the next side job — and we heard everything.

Beni had his guys follow Tony and intercept the job. The only men standing were Tony and his accomplice. Beni wanted them alive. So, they took them to a safe house used for interrogation. Tony was shaking.

"Tony, I'm disappointed in you," Beni began. "I leave you in charge of the NJ office and what do you do? Huh? You double cross me!"

"Look Beni, there's been a mistake. I was going to pass on all the dough. I did good... made extra deals. I did it for you, Beni!"

"Shut the fuck up!" Beni was fuming. "You know what? You're a fucking liar."

Beni turned away, grabbed a chair and sat astride it with his arms resting on the back. "I'm a fortunate man," he said, "I married a very smart woman and she found a whole lot of stuff... money you've been stealing from me. You've been dealing on the side. Not smart, to cut me out."

"So now you have a pussy do your dirty work for you..."

Tony didn't finish his sentence before Beni struck him hard across the face.

"No one talks that way about my wife!" Beni shouted and turning to his men, he issued an order. "Make him talk and when he's done... beat his brain to a pulp."

Beni walked over to Tony and looked into his eyes. "You know our ways... we make an example of those who betray us."

Beni walked to the door and paused. "Get the word out," he said addressing his men, "no one does this to the Sorrentinos and lives. And—" he said, raising his voice, "no one calls the wife of the godfather a *broad*! Ricordare... fedele al giuramento di Omerta!"

With that, Beni left the building.

Tony was never seen again, but word got out — along with the horrific photos of his punishment.

*

Gilda noted my anxiety and paused. "Is this too much for you, Frances?" she asked.

"I was wondering how you coped with the violence," I said.

"I found it difficult. I abhorred the senseless killings. But I had to accept their ways of policing themselves. They couldn't rely on law enforcement to protect their interests. Many of the police were corrupt. They eliminated the bad guys and law enforcement turned a blind eye. Many of them, including judges, were on the pad... paid hush money. They were a law unto themselves. They were ruthless; they granted no exceptions, no second chances. Consequently, no one messed with the Mafia."

Gilda smiled, "Actually, I *did* take a stand against the protection racketeering, because that affected innocent people like my parents. We'll get to that part of my life tomorrow," she said. "And now, Frances dear, I think you need a drink."

Becoming The Mafia Queen
Day Eleven

"Good morning, Frances," Gilda said, greeting me with a glass of fresh orange juice. "I'd like to begin early today, if that's alright with you?"

"Good morning Gilda. Yes, that's fine," and I began recording.

*

After the shake-up with Tony, Beni appointed a new capo to run the NJ faction. He was a trusted made man who had grown up within the *Family.*

I traveled to the States every four months on my own, to see my parents and enjoyed staying in my old room above the jewelry shop. Our Mafia faction protected them well — the irony — no more broken windows, no more terror raids. They were protected from enemy gangs too and most importantly from the developing and ruthless Russian mafia.

They were changed people. The stress had lifted from their faces and they walked with a skip in their step. They frequented kosher restaurants with their Jewish friends, visited the movie theater and even went dancing. It brought me great joy to see them enjoying their lives.

On each occasion, I'd ask them to visit me in Italy, all expenses paid. But they always refused.

"Life is good for us now. We're protected here," Mendel would say. "If we travel to Italy, we'll be with the Mafia and…"

"He doesn't want to mix with them, Gilda," Neta reminded me. "It wouldn't feel right.

We're Jewish, and the Mafia are predominantly Catholic. You understand?"

"Of course. When things are good… you don't change them. Your happiness is mine, too," I'd say. And then I'd kiss them, knowing that we'd repeat this ritual again.

*

I was now regarded as an asset in my own right and not just the godfather's wife. People referred to me as the young Mafia queen; that was preferable to "signora" and carried with it my good reputation. Few women during the last two centuries have had this honor bestowed upon them, and none under the age of fifty.

No one messed with me. I had earned the respect of the NJ faction and our enemies, too. My reputation was built on hard work and fair-minded business practice. I made myself indispensable to our network of clans across the United States and Italy. The associates were a huge source of our business, but as you know, they're not made men: unlike the soldati, they had not taken the oath of Omerta. However, they knew they could trust me, even when deals went bad. I'd trouble-shoot the situation and try to save their necks, before they were separated from their torsos by the trigger-happy soldati. I developed a keen instinct for honesty... I could almost smell it and I acted upon my intuition, which was usually correct.

As I mentioned previously, I kept up with the pace of evolving technology. But I'm getting ahead of myself. It was 1975 and although I was only twenty-eight, I handled those *Family* finances and mundane business deals that Beni and Dino chose to delegate. I was CFO of the Sorrentino *Family* and much, much more.

During the following two years, Beni and I settled into a calmer, happy form of marriage, as couples do when the rose-colored glasses are removed. My trips to the US were frequent and the limoncello and olive oil businesses were yielding good profits.

*

It was during my visit in the fall of 1977 that I confided in my parents.

"I want to put a stop to the racketeering," I told them.

"In our town?" enquired Mendel.

"Not just our town," I replied. "The whole state. I want to wipe it out of New Jersey."

"Gilda, it would be dangerous for you to cross the Mafia," Neta interjected.

Let me ask you why?" said Mendel, giving me a wise look. "You know they'll kill you, if you betray them. So the question is... why would you put yourself at risk?"

"Because innocent people are suffering, just as you did. I'm in a position to stop it... I can help them. Just like I helped free you from a life of misery," I said.

"You're the godfather's wife! You can't go against Beni," Neta pleaded. "And what if you have a baby? Have you considered that?"

"I'm resigned to the fact that I can't have any more children. But I can help the families that *do* have children, and who are persecuted by the Mafia's racketeering operation. They deserve a better life," I said.

"Even if it costs you your own life?" Mendel said.

"Yes," I answered.

"I'm proud of you, Gilda," Mendel said.

"What are you talking Mendel? Do you know what you're saying?" Neta was upset.

"Yes, I know what I'm saying. I often think that if more Jews had stood up to the Nazis, more families would have survived. But the Jews were submissive and so they were overpowered by the Nazi regime."

Mendel had said his piece and Neta was silenced.

"Thank you, Papa," I said. Mendel beamed with pride.

"Ah Gilda, you're a brave, headstrong young woman." Neta walked around the table, sat down beside me and took hold of my hand. "How can we help?" she asked.

"I have to find a person whom I can trust. Maybe someone in the FBI who's willing to work undercover and help me. But if I approach the FBI directly, they'll inform the *Family...* there are many on the payroll," I said.

"We'll ask some of the shopkeepers," Mendel said, "they have friends who want to rid the neighborhood of the Mafia. It's a start Gilda, but it may take some time."

"Be patient Gilda and goodness will prevail." Neta's words sounded profound, but my acquired wisdom had taught me that goodness does *not* always prevail. We would need a lot of luck, too.

*

"Did you realize the consequences of your decision, Gilda?" I asked.

"Of course, but I had to try," she said.

*

My next visit was in April 1978. As soon as I arrived, I checked the accounts in our NJ office and then I was free to join my parents for Passover. I was so excited to be in the States at this time of year. Passover was special and the thought of us three being together filled me with joy.

But the table was set for four. They had invited a new Jewish friend, whose parents were out of town, visiting relatives.

David was polite, educated and in his mid-thirties. He was also single and attractive. But it was the contrast between his dark hair and green eyes that struck me the most. His eyes were magnetic… and I instinctively felt an inexplicable surge of sensuality, which surprised me and caught me off guard. But I was quick to disengage for fear of being lured into an entanglement.

My parents had come to include him in their lives on a regular basis and I struggled with the thought that he might be a substitute for me. Later, I was to learn otherwise.

We talked and I asked him what he did for a living. There was an uncomfortable silence. David glanced sideways at Mendel and then told me he worked in law enforcement. Neta starred at me and then unnaturally stated that David was "a trusted friend". It took me a while to catch on.

"David's mother and I are friends," Neta spoke out. "We belong to the same Jewish Women's Circle. We got talking about the racketeering in our neighborhood and she mentioned that her son, David, was trying to eradicate this operation. But, there were too many bad cops on the Mafia's payroll."

"We need someone on the inside… a person we can trust," said David. "The clans are tight, so they're impossible to infiltrate. We've been looking for a man…"

"Or woman!" Mendel interjected. "I'm going to speak boldly," he said. "Gilda, you may be the person they've been waiting for."

"Mendel, I trust *you* with all my heart, but can I be sure?"

"Yes Gilda. David is trustworthy. I would stake my life on it. And Gilda my dear, you know that I would *never* place your life at risk."

"This is the chance you've been waiting for," Neta said.

David turned his chair towards mine. "Gilda, we've been searching for an insider… a man who'd turn on the Sorrentino faction," David paused and stared at me. "But I never considered the possibility of a woman!"

"Are you aware that I'm the godfather's wife?"

"Yes, of course. We've been watching you since you connected with Beni," he said. "When you married into the Sorrentino *Family*, you became a high priority."

"So you must also know that I'm not gonna snitch on my *Family*… particularly my husband."

David looked puzzled. "I was told you wanted to stop the protection racket?" he said.

"I do… but that's *all* I want to stop. If I co-operate, you don't touch my *Family*," I demanded.

"Okay, you have my word," he promised.

I studied his face long and hard. "You're obviously aware that my men are watching every move I make. So, aren't you afraid?" I asked.

"No, because I have your parents as my cover," he replied.

"How dare you place them at risk by befriending them and coming to this house!" I was angry. David immediately pushed his chair away from the table and stood up to leave.

"Stop!" I said. "I want to know — what's in it for you?"

"Gilda…"

"Quiet Mendel, I know what I'm doing," I snapped.

"It's personal," David replied.

"So you're not just a vigilante, taking the law into your own hands? You have some skin in the game… please share the reason you'd risk your life, so I can calibrate your authenticity."

"Gilda…" Mendel tried again to interject.

"Please Mendel, let me handle this. Our lives depend on my assessment," I stated.

Mendel and Neta looked shocked by my speech. They'd never seen me in full Mafia mode — and I was now a pro.

David sat down again and staring at the kitchen table throughout, he began to relay his reasons.

"It was five years ago when I first set eyes on Hannah. She and her parents were new to the neighborhood and I remember how she stood out in the crowd of women at temple. She was strikingly beautiful, with dark hair and green eyes and a radiance which seemed to glow from within. We fell in love and became engaged to be married. Her father had bought the gun store, on the adjacent street…"

"There's no gun store there," I interjected.

"No, not anymore." David paused and swallowed hard, to keep his emotions in check, before he continued. "Her father and brothers ran the business and Hannah kept the books. The brothers began dealing with the Mafia… selling them guns, and more. Eventually, they became greedy and double-crossed them by trading with rival gangs. The Mafia hit them… killed them in the street outside the store. They took the father and tortured him and the mother…" David wiped a tear from his eye, "the mother and Hannah disappeared overnight. I searched across the States, until I eventually found them hiding in New Mexico. The mother is a broken woman and Hannah is confined to a mental institution. She's suffering from catatonic depression, which is so severe as to render her uncommunicative. She doesn't recognize me."

Neta leaned forward and touched David gently on his hand. "Gilda, it wasn't the Sorrentino faction that did this," she explained.

"I'm sorry for your sadness," I told David. "But unless I verify your story, I can't risk working with you."

"Then I'll give you their names and the newspaper article. You can also contact the institution... or I could take you."

"I can't go there with you, but give me everything you have," I said. "Then I'll consider if your word is trustworthy."

Neta interjected, "It's Passover, shall we begin now?"

We all agreed and I sat down with my beloved parents and David — who was either genuine or a fraud. I wasn't sure which.

*

"Frances, let me explain the risk. I was very afraid that David had been planted by one of our NJ faction members as a trick to remove me, after we'd rid ourselves of Tony," Gilda confessed. "I was also afraid they'd kill Mendel and Neta."

"So, what did you do?" I asked.

"I studied all the available evidence and checked out the article in the newspaper. I then met with the newly-appointed boss of our NJ office to discuss the current state of my parents' protection. I guessed that they were surveying all their visitors and told him I wanted an update. He showed me a report, which verified that David Czarnowski had been investigated and was indeed the son of Neta's friend. The boss explained everything.

"Their friends are mainly couples, except for the Czarnowskis, they have a son. He's a nancy boy... you know, homo." He cleared his throat in embarrassment.

"Homosexual?"

"Yeah... that's it," he said. "The loner type."

"Definitely not interested in women, then?"

"Look, if he were... we'd have Beni on our case. We got instructions... he don't want you alone with other men, but this guy? Well he's a..."

"Okay, I get it. Thanks." I said.

"Signora Sorrentino, your parents are safe with us. No one's gonna get 'em on my watch... capisce?"

"Capisco," I replied. But now I was totally confused. David had relayed a sob story about his girlfriend. Was he lying?

*

"Are you hungry, Frances?" Gilda asked.

"Yes…" Before I could finish my sentence, the housekeeper came bustling into the room with two irresistible antipasto salads. We devoured them, along with sweet memories of Italy, before we resumed for the afternoon session.

*

At first I disliked David and he felt the same about me. Neither of us completely trusted the other. I found him arrogant and he did not understand how I could condone the Mafia lifestyle. There was definite friction between us, which became all too clear during our next meeting.

"How could you live with the godfather of the Sorrentino Mafia?" David asked.

"He's my husband. Beni's a goodhearted man."

"How can you say that Gilda? He's Mafia!" David was incensed.

"He's good and kind to his immediate Italian family… and that includes me," I explained. "He inherited the position of joint head of the Sorrentino Mafia clan after his uncle was brutally murdered. His loyalty to the *Family* made him accept that position, which carries much responsibility and danger." I said.

"That violent brutality is exactly what I'm talking about Gilda. How can you condone it?"

"I don't. I dislike the violence and cruelty, but you must remember that the Mafia are self-policing and when they're attacked, they retaliate. They avenge their enemies. You're Jewish, David, you were taught to believe that an eye for an eye and a tooth for a tooth is acceptable in Jewish law. That clearly condones retaliation," I stated.

"In my world, the law prohibits that behavior," David said.

"And in my world, it's different," I said.

"You live in a Mafia compound!" David was now irate.

"I live under the protection of the Mafia because I married the godfather," I answered sharply. "Because I had to!"

David was silent for a minute. "So — leave," he said.

"I can never leave. I made a deal."

"A deal with the devil."

"If you're going to trivialize my decision, *you* can leave — now," I told him.

"I apologize, Gilda," David said. "Please go on."

"I made a deal with Beni to release my parents from the protection racket," I explained. "The Mafia don't collect from their own family and that includes their spouses' families too."

"Now, I understand. I'm sorry Gilda. I won't mention it again," David said.

"Beni kept his promise. He's loyal and so am I. But my loyalty stops in NJ and that's why I'm contemplating working with you, to prevent further racketeering," I said, feeling quite exhausted by the intensity of our conversation.

We sat in silence and drank some coffee. Neither initiated conversation after our shark-like exchange.

"It's convenient that we'll be able to conduct our work sessions here. It'll avoid undue attention," David said.

"It's essential to work in this house," I replied. "It would be disastrous to collaborate elsewhere." He was stating the obvious, the alternative would be stupid.

"Good," he said. "We'll begin tomorrow, after breakfast."

"What time will you arrive?" I asked.

"Gilda, I'm living in this house," David said.

"Since when?" I was stunned.

"Since today," he replied. "I had to confirm that we'd be working together before I moved back to this area."

"But I thought you lived with your parents?" I said.

"My parents only have a small apartment. Mendel and Neta suggested I lodge with them. I'm a paying guest." He smiled smugly and awaited my response.

"Make sure not to bring your boyfriends back to this house. My parents would be greatly offended," I stated.

"*What?*" he said, looking confused.

"I'm told you're homosexual," I said, using the formal term.

David laughed out loud before answering. "I've heard that the modern term nowadays is gay. And I'm most definitely not gay."

Once again he'd surprised me; I felt mentally disheveled by his remarks. "I don't know what to say, I was told on good authority. If I offended you, I'm sorry."

"Don't be. If I were gay, I wouldn't hesitate to tell you. I'm an honest, open kinda guy and I told you about Hannah, my fiancée." He spoke genuinely and this time I was acquiescent.

"So, I guess we're housemates," I said, holding out my hand in a gesture of friendship.

"I guess so," he replied, taking my hand firmly in his, but squeezing it gently.

It was then I became infused with mixed emotions. I was pleased that he seemed a kind person who'd be living with Neta and Mendel. But also, I was afraid he might draw their affection away from me. I'd lost one set of parents and I didn't want to lose another.

*

Beni always referred to David as "that homo surrogate", that Mendel and Neta had adopted as a substitute for me. It was a crude and hurtful assumption. David was straight; he liked women, but avoided relationships due to his involvement in covert operations. The NJ boss had created a ruse which we didn't deny. It was a convenient cover and Beni never suspected the truth. Mendel and Neta were amused by Beni's assumption, but understood that it served our purpose. They were never at risk. Being Jewish, they knew how to keep secrets.

*

Beni had the NJ faction protect me too. They would collect me from the airport and deliver me to my parents' home, then they'd ostensibly leave me alone. But they were always watching the house. I felt quite safe… they guarded me with their lives. I was the godfather's wife and treated with respect. More importantly, I was the last person they'd suspect of betrayal.

*

I had vowed to abolish the protection racketeering from NJ, but, I grossly underestimated the enormity of the task. The RICO act had been passed in 1970. RICO means Racketeer Influenced and Corrupt Organizations Act — it's a federal law, designed to combat organized crime in the United States. But there was a big problem. Corrupt officers within law enforcement, government officials and members of the judicial system were all paid to ignore racketeering, which included extortion. They were on the pad, in other words, they were receiving tax-free handouts from the Mafia. The first part of my plan was to check the accounts in our NJ office and match the names of the culprits to the illicit payments. I managed all the accounts, so I was aware of the fraud.

David was working with an undercover group in special operations, a branch of the FBI. I passed on the information I discovered to David, who set a false trail of evidence, which suggested that there was a mole within law enforcement who was informing on his colleagues. The Mafia payoffs were sent to one central bank, where the FBI traced other payments from the Russian mafia and rival Italian gangs, too.

The accounts were frozen, followed by several arrests. This clever process was to set rival gangs at each other's throats. Not only were they competing for territory... let me explain. Territory not only refers to a district, but also to an underworld jurisdiction where extortion rackets are officially designated as belonging to a *Family*. Therefore, each gang thought that the other had a rat amongst them, who was passing information to the FBI. There was much blood spilled on the streets as each gang gunned down the other in assaults during protection collections. Consequently, the gangs had to cut back their extortion due to loss of manpower.

David and I needed a code phrase and so I chose *Open Sesame*, which Mendel and I had agreed upon during my wedding.

We managed to clean up almost all the districts and eliminate those law enforcement officers who were illegally receiving pay-offs to ignore criminal activity. Together, David and I were responsible for weeding out a number of corrupt cops, government officials and judges. In court they sang like birds, which led to arrests of Mafia gang members, including some of our own soldiers who were double trading.

We also targeted the corruption within the big unions. The term was ghost payroll, and it applied to non-existent or no-show employees who were added to a payroll through a corrupt labor union, in order to funnel money to the Mafia.

The Russian mafia was the cruelest of all the gangs and although their numbers were growing at an alarming rate due to increased immigration, the FBI managed to successfully curtail their operations. I continued working to expose the Russian operatives in NJ. Factions were now using computers, so I became an expert and checked all computer records that were linked to our NJ office. The boss of the NJ faction struggled with computers and mainly left paper trails. Both were useful. I devised financial files, kept track of our accounts and more.

*

"Gilda," I asked, "did these orchestrated tip-offs coincide with your visits?"

"That's a good point. We actually staggered the inside information, to confuse and distract them from any connection to me," Gilda said.

"Didn't Beni look for the informant?"

"Of course, and that's why I inserted names of fictitious associates into the accounts. I then accused the NJ boss of dealing with outsiders, who probably caused the leaks." Gilda replied.

"That's clever, but Gilda, didn't anyone suspect you? You were the one person responsible for the accounting in the NJ office."

"I was the only person in the Sorrentino *Family* who understood the accounts," Gilda laughed. "The Data Encryption Standard (DES) is a block cipher; a form of shared secret encryption. It was selected by the National Bureau of Standards as an official Federal Information Processing Standard (FIPS) for the United States in 1976. My way of securing the accounts was to encrypt them."

"*Encryption*? Nonno was right when he stated that you were smarter than all the *Family* including his grandsons," I said, laughing too.

"I was playing a dangerous game, so I made myself indispensable. I was a childless wife; therefore I was afforded the privilege of working. The Sorrentino *Family* business grew exponentially while I was the financial controller."

"So you and David became friends?" I asked.

"Oh, we were *much* more," she answered and I noticed that her eyes glazed over when she spoke of him.

"Gilda, I have a personal question about David." I said.

"Did I have an affair with him? Yes, I did... it was sweet and tender and a very long time ago. Don't think badly of me. I was childless and in Italy the men stray, particularly when there are no children. My husband and his twin enjoyed time with their lovers, but they also respected me and recognized my value," Gilda added, as if to compensate for her adultery.

"I completely understand," I said.

"Remember, I was a Mafia queen and not at liberty to love another man."

"And did you Gilda? Did you love him?"

"Oh yes... he was the love of my life. Our love was that rare kind of love, that surpasses all time and distance. Our separation was difficult to endure, but it never changed our relationship. After several months of being apart, we'd continue as if it were yesterday. We worked together for several years denying our love. He was honorable; I was a married woman. It was I who eventually made the first move towards intimacy," Gilda admitted. "But I'm getting ahead of myself and I need to stop now. I have another appointment today."

Memories Of Love
Day Twelve

"Good morning Gilda," I said, greeting her at breakfast. "Whatever are you drinking?" I asked, staring at the container of green-colored liquid in her hand.

"It's a nutritional shake, prescribed by my doctor. I'm trying to boost my immune system," she explained. "Although the color is a little off-putting."

"Are you ill?" I asked.

"I'm well enough to face another day of storytelling," she replied, avoiding a direct answer.

I had noticed that Gilda's energy levels were decreasing, but hadn't mentioned it. "Best close your eyes and pretend it's champagne," I suggested.

*

I'd just arrived back in the US after a particularly turbulent time in my marriage. The year was 1983, I was thirty-six years old and I was hurting.

Beni had been seeing other women for the previous five years. It was accepted as a normal progression of marriage in Italy and it made no difference that I was married to the godfather. Other wives within our clan had also endured their husbands' infidelities. We were expected not to make a fuss and I was no exception to the rule. It was the 1980s and very much a man's world, particularly in Italy. But Beni's latest affair had consequences that I'd not expected.

I joined David the next morning, eager to bury my emotional pain in work. But he saw through my facade.

"What's up?" he enquired, looking at me intensely with those magnetic eyes.

"Nothing," I said, trying to avoid his question.

He walked around the table and placed his hands on my shoulders.

"Gilda, I know you... we've worked together for five years. I can tell that something's wrong." he said.

I kept my head lowered, trying not to look directly into David's eyes. He gently lifted my chin with his fingers and he could see that I was beginning to cry.

"Oh Gilda," he said, "I'm here for you." And he held me until I felt calm enough to speak.

We sat together and I began to unburden my problem. "Beni's having an affair... it's not the first, but this time — she's pregnant," The words stumbled clumsily out of my mouth. "Beni and I can't have children."

"And you assumed it was his fault?"

"No, I knew the truth. It was me. But, I wanted everyone else to assume..."

"I understand. So you and Beni chose not to tell the family you couldn't have children?" David suggested.

"It's worse than that... I hid the truth from Beni. I had to let him believe we'd have children, or he'd never have married me," I confessed. "It was to protect my parents."

"I understand why you had to lie. But are you sure you can't conceive?"

I looked at him and took a deep breath before I spoke. "David, I know I can trust you, so I'm going to tell you everything. I have a son."

I told him all about Gary, the adoption and the terrible abusive attack that I'd suffered at Michael Allen's hands. When I finished my story, I felt relieved. But David looked horrified.

"I had no idea of the pain you'd encountered. This man, Michael Allen is a monster! I want to kill him!"

"That is something I have to do myself," I said, "I'm serious, David. I want him to look into my eyes and know the pain of death. But first, I'll have to find him."

"Let me help." His offer was genuine. "I traced Hannah... I've contacts...".

"Thanks David, I'm grateful for your support. It's a daunting task to undertake alone and I don't want the Mafia involved, as Beni must never know about my son. It's my secret—"

"*Our* secret, and it's safe with me," David said.

I leaned forward to thank him with a kiss on the cheek, but somehow he turned his head and our lips met. That first kiss was sweet and tender and it needn't have gone further. We could have settled for friendship... if the passion had not been present. But it was. It was I who initiated the next move. I kissed him again and all our suppressed feelings exploded. The past five years of friendship had developed into a sensual embrace from which there was no return.

"I never want to leave you Gilda," he whispered. "All these lonely years of watching you, loving you… waiting until you visited again. I love you Gilda… I've always loved you."

In that moment, I wasn't sure if I felt love for David or just needed to *be* loved. I was living in the present and our work, the Mafia and the fact that I was married… none of that seemed to matter.

Then we heard Neta's footsteps on the stairs and scrambled to distance ourselves by sitting apart, across the kitchen table. But the tension was dynamic, as though an electric field had formed an arc which leapt between our bodies, binding us together. Neta was an astute woman and I'm sure she felt the atmosphere and noticed the glow in my cheeks. But she was also discreet, and quickly busied herself elsewhere.

We tried desperately to work for a couple of hours and then we both went our separate ways. I visited the NJ office and concentrated on the accounts. David went to his HQ.

We met again at the dinner table, joined by Neta and Mendel. I think we tried too hard not to let our newfound excitement show, that we almost seemed aloof. But once my parents had gone to bed, the fireworks began.

I quietly let David into my room and secured the latch. The reality of our situation was laid bare. We knew we were crossing boundaries and that this affair would not end well, but neither of us could stop this force… it was overwhelming.

I turned on my TV to cover the sound of our voices, should we lose control. We stood face to face and discarded our robes and he gently lowered me on to the bed. We lay together and touched each other's skin, as though it were a gift. Then, with accelerated excitement we tossed and turned, lost in the joy of sizzling sensuality. I'd never experienced such complete and utter joy. I'd only had two lovers before and now, at the age of thirty-six, I was experiencing the fusion of physical and mental emotion for the first time in my life.

I was in love… but with a man I couldn't keep. It was bitter-sweet.

David released a passion in me that I didn't know existed. I'd never felt this intensity with Beni. Our marriage consisted of a different kind of love, based on friendship and obligation. It really was a contract to benefit us both. I think I just accepted that it was God's way of rescuing my parents from persecution. I was so grateful to Neta and Mendel for a second chance in life, that I'd have done anything to help them.

*

"Frances, I need a moment… these memories…" Without finishing her sentence, she let her head fall forward and closed her eyes.

"Would you like a glass of water?" I asked, after an interval.

"Yes, thank you Frances." She sipped the water slowly as if she were cleansing her memories, one by one.

*

During this phase I lived a double life. I alternated between two men… one was my husband and the other my lover. Separation between the two was essential for my mind and heart; my brain operated in Italy, but my heart resided in America. My life was split between working against the Mafia and working for the Mafia. It was a complicated existence, which I continued for many years.

*

During the early 1980s, a strong Italian Mafia faction was emerging in Sicily. The self-appointed godfather was born in the small town of Gondo and after many years on the mainland, he returned and adopted the name of the town as his own.

He brought with him thugs he'd collected over the years. They were loyal, ambitious and brutal. The Gondo faction wiped out the opposing clans in Sicily, beginning with the rightful godfathers and their sons, progressing to the capos and soldati. Gondo also murdered the mayors and many police. The Sicilian people were living under a reign of terror, controlled by a vicious tyrant.

The established Mafia *Families* across Italy honored a code of conduct between clans. There was respect for the dynasties and a line drawn between *Family* members and business. Gondo was different: disrespectful and a power-seeking psychopath. He was highly intelligent but uneducated, and his behavior erratic and spontaneous. We heard that he was terrifying to be around, even his family were fearful of saying the wrong word, or suggesting something that he disliked, as this would trigger a shooting. He had no restraint and would kill on impulse. It took only six months for Gondo to rule Sicily and after that, he set his sights on claiming the Italian mainland.

In 1984, Dino and Beni called for un incontro dei padrini… a meeting of the godfathers. The venue and surrounding location were classified as top secret and the subject was Gondo.

The heads of the six most prestigious clans in Italy gathered together, along with lesser clans. The commission, consisting of the seven Mafia bosses from New York had also agreed to attend, as the core of the Families, which had been established over the last two centuries, still resided in Italy. The survival of the Families was paramount to the Mafia retaining power around the world. Their respect for one another was key to their working collectively to combat this ambitious psychopath, Gondo.

Once the arrangements were set, Beni and Dino traveled within a heavily armed convoy of capos and soldati. The venue was an old farmhouse, which had belonged to an ancestor of one of the godfathers. The security was a joint collaboration and tighter than ever before. No one could breach the mile wide circle which surrounded the farmhouse, particularly the polizia. We even had machine guns positioned on high points to guard against an air attack. There were numerous soldati spaced out at checkpoints along the roads leading to the venue… it was impregnable.

*

"Gilda, did you attend the meeting?" I asked.

"No, Frances. As a mere woman, I was not permitted to attend. I stayed at home with Nonno and a necessary home guard. We knew, through our networks, that word of this historic meeting had reached Gondo in Sicily and his retaliation was likely. He had been shunned by the highest Mafia bosses and he would likely choose this time to attack, while our guard was under-armed. We lived in the region of Campania. If Gondo was planning an attack, he would hit the Nadranetta clan first, in the region of Calabria. They were especially vulnerable, being located so close to Sicily," Gilda said. "But, if he was as cunning as we believed, he'd take advantage of both Families being under-guarded and he'd hit us both on the same night."

"Were you afraid?"

"Yes. Gondo's violent reputation preceded him," Gilda stated, "and his methods were barbaric."

"Gilda, after all these years living with the Mafia, you must have been prepared for violent raids such as these?"

"Yes Frances, unfortunately I saw much violence, it was an ugly part of our lives. But this man was especially brutal. He would torture and kill children. The established Families abided by a code of conduct. The order for a hit was issued as a revenge tactic, it was business. Gondo was a psychopath, intent on killing every living thing that prevented his becoming the capo di tutti capi," Gilda said, looking disgusted.

"I remember transcribing the horrific story of how Beni's uncle was assassinated, along with his wife and children. The killers were Mafiosi too, so surely they were just as evil as Gondo?" I suggested.

"You're right, Frances. It was an evil revenge killing by a clan whom Beni's uncle had hurt financially," she said, "and sometimes the Mafiosi go on a killing spree and that sets in motion continuous acts of revenge. But the killings are revenge-induced and we all try to live by the code, Omerta, because it's at times such as these that we need to support one another," Gilda explained.

*

While the meeting was in full play, Nonno and I sat together in the upstairs living room. We were armed and had a soldato outside our door. Nonno was old and his hands shook but I still gave him his gun. It was a matter of pride. I was a good shot... I'd been trained well.

Beni wanted to send me away to a safe house, with Dino's wife and children, but Nonno was too ill to travel and I wouldn't leave him. I had a bed brought upstairs for Nonno and positioned near the bathroom. I arranged for his nurse to sleep in the next room and I sat in a chair, watchful and vigilant as always.

*

At the meeting, Dino spoke first. "Gondo is already penetrating the mainland. We need collective intelligence in place... we must know where he is at all times of the day and night."

"He must be taken out... exterminated," said Beni, "before a bloodbath ensues. His pattern is to hit the Mayor of the towns first, followed by the police and judges, but he's unpredictable. He could be attacking our homes as we speak. Capisce?"

"Si capisco," each agreed.

"He's coming for our wives and children—"

"We need to act now!"

"He'll come after the godfathers next," said the underboss from the Genovetti *Family.*

"I propose we hit him in Sicily."

"I hear he wants the title of capo di tutti capi," said the godfather of the Colombo *Family*

"Fat fucking chance!"

"That don't exist no more," said our consigliere.

The Colombo godfather spoke up again. "His goal is to overrun us and resurrect this position for himself. Over my dead body!"

"It might be… don't tempt fate," replied Dino.

"We need to stand together against this monster," said the godfather of the Maglioni clan. We need to protect our wives and children… think about the future."

"They are our future," said Beni. "We're an institution… our families have held these domains for centuries. It's our duty to preserve our heritage."

The oldest godfather stood to speak. "Strategy is the key. This low life is cunning, but we're educated, smart and the wisdom of our forefathers pulses in our veins. We can outwit and outnumber him… we're strong if we stand together. So I say we lay aside our personal animosities, forget our grievances and together we conquer this animal, before he destroys us. Have no doubt, he means to butcher our families and wipe us off the face of this earth! This is not business… this is personal."

The speech by this respected capo di capi was applauded by all; they voted in agreement to eliminate Gondo and detailed each clan's duties.

The meeting had been challenging and all were hungry. It must have been an awesome sight, to view these godfathers feasting together in peace.

But the peace was soon broken, when a message arrived informing them of an attack on the Nadranetta clan's home base. As they feared, Gondo had hit them when and where they were most vulnerable — in the region of Calabria, closest to Sicily.

Beni and Dino left immediately. Their drive south was arduous. The route to Sorrento was fraught with twists and turns that only an experienced driver could navigate in daytime… this was night. There were no lights, not even the moon, as they travelled the winding road along the cliffs to Sorrento.

Both men sat in silence, each analyzing possible scenarios. This was a time before mobile phones and their car sped faster than a single soldado carrying a written message.

*

It was around midnight when I heard the first blast. It was near our main gate and it activated the alarms. Automatic lights illuminated the drive and the perimeter of the house. I heard shouting and then gunshots.

Nonno was asleep. I chose not to wake him at this time. When the nurse came running into the room, I calmed her and told her to sit silently beside Nonno, but not to wake him. I loaded my gun and listened. There was another blast as explosives were hurled towards the house. We'd recently armed our men with brand new Sterling submachine guns. They fire from an open bolt, but in trained hands, their accuracy is perfect. I watched from my window as they took down six aggressors. Then followed that eerie silence. A time to flirt with death, gauge who's left alive and who could take you out. A hand must have twitched on a corpse below our window, for one of our soldati to unload his round.

We waited for what seemed like hours, but only minutes had passed. Then, the men cautiously approached the bodies and with their SMG barrels aimed at the aggressors' heads, they flipped them over with their feet. None showed any sign of life.

Then, suddenly, we heard the engines of our cars as they came roaring through the open gates. Beni's car stopped outside the main door and as he looked up, we locked eyes. His relief was obvious and he blew me a kiss, before he ascended the stairs.

I was comforting Nonno when Beni entered the living room. He walked over to us and placed his arms around both our shoulders.

"I'm so sorry," he said, as tears began to run down his cheeks.

We just held on to each other, pleased we were all alive.

*

"Gilda?" I spoke her name softly, but she didn't hear. "Gilda?" I said again, "shall we stop for lunch?"

"Sorry Frances, my mind was elsewhere. Yes, lunch would be good," she said with a sigh.

*

In spite of the attacks on us and on the Nadranetta compound, the grand meeting of the godfathers was deemed a success. But although the clans stood together against the Sicilian, there followed a violent and bloody Mafia power struggle. Gondo would stop at nothing, including assassinating the police and kidnapping children. Some of his Mafiosi couldn't stomach his violent methods, so when Mario Mannrella, Gondo's right hand man, decided to testify against Gondo in court and provide evidence, others followed his example. Twenty Mafiosi were charged with seventy-nine murders and given life sentences. The courts went crazy as Mafiosi came forward to testify… it had never happened on such a scale before.

But most devastating was the testimony from Mario Mannrella himself. His testimony brought down over three hundred men, including a number of high ranking politicians, lawyers and police captains.

Gondo was losing control. His threats to kill *Family* members of the men who'd turned against him, were not enough to stop the onslaught of Mafiosi testifying.

*

"Do you know Frances, there is an unwritten code of honor among the Mafia, that if Mafiosi go to prison, their families are looked after for life."

"Did Gondo abide by this code?" I asked Gilda.

"Oh no, he did far worse. Those who turned against Gondo and broke loyalty with him, paid dearly," she said.

*

Gondo's Mafiosi were declining, through killings and police arrests. He decided to deliver a punishment that would prove so severe as to deter any more from defecting.

In the November of 1989, Mario Mannrella's mother and two sisters had planned to travel to stay with family near Bologna. As they left their home by car, three black sedans ambushed it. With the use of a rifle and three revolvers, Gondo's men ripped off the back door of the women's car and fired inside. The women were riddled with bullets… they died in agony.

Never before had the Mafia murdered women for the disloyalty of a Mafioso. But instead of inciting fear, Gondo's act of vengeance caused a wave of disgust. There was always the danger of retaliation… that's what the Mafia do. But this time it was different. Mafiosi in their hundreds began revealing what they knew to the prosecutors who were pursuing Gondo. This revelation continued over several years. It was astounding! Gondo fought back and, due to his connections, managed to stay out of jail.

The other clans abhorred Gondo's violence towards women and children. They were also, collectively, losing money. Gondo was tying up the drugs trade. He'd obtained a pledge from the cartel of drug-traffickers in Colombia. To give you an idea of the profits back in the 1980s, each purchase of 1,300 pounds of cocaine would cost $3 million, from which Gondo would make a profit of $16 million. This was from just one shipment! Can you imagine what he made annually? The other clans were cut out of these deals and there was growing resentment.

Personally, I hated the drug trafficking, but I wasn't about to turn Beni over to the law. And besides, the law was on the pad. There'd always been competition between the six clans but, usually there was enough profit to support all the Families across Italy. By this time, Gondo's greed had sucked up most of the business and competition became fierce. The clans began to turn on one another in an effort to fight his monopoly. Consequently, the pledge to work together ruptured.

There were two judges who'd been particularly persistent. For three consecutive years they'd worked together to try to bring Gondo to justice. They wanted a trial… it would have been the trial of the century, if only they had succeeded. The biggest problem was the collusion between the politicians, police captains and the Mafia. Gondo had them all on his payroll.

Gondo had a particular hatred for one judge in particular. His name was Judge Falcini. He was aggressively pursuing the heads of all the Mafia, but his first and foremost goal was Gondo. In 1990, Judge Falcini was up for promotion. He was next in line to become the chief prosecutor. This was dangerous for us, due to the judge's friendship with the Attorney General of New Jersey, which had already led to arrests in both New Jersey and New York of people with links to the Sorrentino *Family*.

The Sicilian Mafia issued a vendetta against Judge Falcini and the politicians were influenced to vote against the judge and unjustly attack his credibility to serve. The Palace of Justice in Rome, which was referred to as the "palace of poisons", was alive with gossip; slanderous comments and unfounded personal allegations. Judge Sellino was the only friend and colleague that stood with Judge Falcini and he too was now a marked man.

The Sicilian Mafia had planned an explosion of epic proportion. One of Gondo's Mafiosi was an explosives expert. He packed thirteen metal drums with 770 pounds of explosives. All the drums, weighing 55 pounds each except for one, which was 77 pounds, were placed under a motorway bridge.

On May 2, 1990, Judge Falcini and his wife boarded an unscheduled flight from Rome to Naples. Their trip, to a safe location, was top secret, but Gondo had received advanced intelligence, and he was waiting for them.

The judge and his wife were riding in their armor-plated car, wedged between two escorts. A convoy of three cars travelled along the motorway, heading down the coast. There was no alternative route around the bridge and so it was an obvious choice for the assassination.

When the convoy crossed the bridge, Gondo's Mafioso flipped the switch via remote control, which triggered the explosion. The blast was so huge, that people thought there'd been an earthquake! It was a terrible mess. They killed not only the judge, but his poor wife and their bodyguards too.

We all knew that Gondo was responsible for Judge Falcini's, assassination, but he put out the word among his corrupt politicians that it was the work of the Sorrentino Mafia.

*

"Oh Gilda! So they thought it was Dino and Beni?"

"Oh, yes. There were several reasons; the murder happened in our domain and Judge Falcini was working with the Attorney General of New Jersey, which impacted our business in the US," Gilda explained. "It was easy to influence the politicians to point the finger at us… they were getting paid big money."

"What did you do?" I asked.

"Beni and Dino placed our home in lockdown and they hit the mattresses. I wasn't allowed to travel to the US for six months, which meant I couldn't see my parents or be with David. It was a difficult period in my life."

Gilda sighed, and continued.

*

The judge's murder caused chaos amongst the Mafia clans right across Italy. I heard through my network that rival clans were also leaking false information to the authorities that suggested it was the work of the Sorrentinos. Big problems were brewing across the mainland, and we were headed for more bloodshed. Gondo had done a fine job of turning the clans against one another — so I decided to implement a fix.

Firstly, I tipped off the police and gave them information on the rival faction's tax evasion the Italian authorities are *very* hot on tax fraud. Then I paid the local mayor and the polizia with commodities for their families: in return came the assurance that we were no longer suspects. I'd worked hard at securing a good reputation with the local authorities and ironically, being a woman gave me an advantage and my word was good. For these reasons, they trusted me.

The assassination of Judge Sellino soon followed. He'd been a close friend of Judge Falcini, and intended to complete the clean-up task that Falcini left unfinished. Again, the finger was pointed at us by Gondo and the spineless clans who assisted this abomination.

I again paid off the local Mayor and the polizia, who graciously turned a blind eye to the massacre that followed, due to our retaliation. The authorities moved quickly to scoop up the remaining casualties of the opposing clans and prosecuted them for murder and fraud. It was a huge triumph for the local dignitaries, who were rewarded by their superiors and won favor in the upper echelons of the hierarchical government system. It was a win-win situation for all.

*

"Oh Gilda, how did you deal with the bloodshed, the violence?"

"Frances, I was part of the Sorrentino *Family*. There were women and children to protect. It was them or us. Tribal instincts kick in when your backs are slammed against the wall. And the only way out is forwards," she said. "You too have experienced this."

"Yes Gilda, I remember only too well," I agreed.

*

I'd become accustomed to the Mafia's way of life. In Italy, you don't involve the polizia without pay-offs. Everyone is on the *take* and everyone gets a share of a pay-off. This is how the Italian government works and the country runs smoothly with the Mafia's assistance.

Dino would become over enthusiastic at times. If things didn't go smoothly people would get killed, and often it wasn't their fault. He liked to make an example of those men who disobeyed or messed up. This is where I had some power. I built my own network of trusted men who would lay down their lives for me, because I protected their wives and children. If I thought Dino was unjust, I'd call them in and tip them off. A lot of lives were saved.

*

What I'm about to divulge might be shocking to most, but this is how the Mafia operates. They have a philosophy; loyalty is paramount and disloyalty is punished severely. After a first insubordination the punishment would fit the crime... similar to an eye for an eye and a tooth for a tooth. For example, if an Associate had his hand in the cookie jar — meaning cash — they'd cut his hand off. After a second offence, they'd kill him.

It was worse for the Mafiosi, who had taken the oath of Omerta. They had no second chances and paid with their lives. It was brutal execution. I abhorred this practice and never condoned it. I would argue the point with Beni, who always insisted that it secured the loyalty of the men. He would remind me that in the Middle East, where they practice this law, there is little crime committed.

The Mafia's revenue came from cocaine and heroin trafficking, counterfeiting, illegal gambling, gun-running, fraud, theft, labor racketeering, loan sharking, illegal immigration, kidnapping, but we didn't touch the white slave industry. I had some clout and I would not allow it.

I have a list of crimes committed by the Mafia in Italy and the US. All are unsolved to this day, due to pay-offs. But I have the evidence and all the names: politicians, lawyers, police chiefs and government officials. All who were on the pad. Once this list goes public, they'll have a field day cleaning up the officials and the other clans.

*

"Gilda, are you sure you want to include the list?" I questioned.

"Yes, I'm quite sure. This book lays open my soul," Gilda replied. "It's my book of revelations and the list must be included."

"But Gilda," I said, feeling quite alarmed by her recklessness, "this sounds extremely dangerous! When Beni and Dino read the book they'll learn that you betrayed them and they'll..."

"Kill me?" She finished my sentence. "Dino will certainly want to, but Beni won't be a problem."

"Aren't you afraid?"

"No. I didn't take the oath of Omerta. Do you know why, Frances?" Gilda said, quite confidently.

"Because Omerta was only for the made men? " I suggested.

"Correct," she said. "Although I rose to the position of Mafia queen and held the power of their finances in my head... no one considered that I should take the oath. Those powerful godfathers overlooked that crucial point, because in their eyes I was a mere woman!" Gilda laughed.

"Frances, I can see them now, clamoring to buy the book and lamenting their stupidity."

*

After the racketeering was cleared from my parents' district, I still needed Beni to honor our agreement to leave my parents alone, without the fear of persecution. I honored my side of the agreement, too, until my parents' death. For many years I sacrificed my independence, but there were compensations. I had money and a beautiful home in Italy, and I devised a way to make myself indispensable to the *Family* by controlling their finances. They didn't expect that from a woman... it took them by surprise. Particularly as they realized that I was not only smarter than the other women, but the men too. That is how I survived.

I appeared to condone Mafia crimes so as to be revered as trustworthy. It earned me the elevated and unique position of Mafia queen for the Sorrentino faction. With that, came power to elicit change.

*

"Frances, I'm quite tired now. This is a good juncture for us to pause until tomorrow."

Endings
Day Thirteen

The Mafia doesn't forget and it doesn't forgive. Beni and Dino were relentless in their quest to reverse the opinion of the prosecutors and to point them towards Gondo.

They once again reached out to the other clans for help. All had suffered financially, due to Gondo's monopolization of the drug-trafficking through Colombia. There were other losses, too. The Sicilian had disrupted the financial agreements between the godfathers and stolen their basic sources of income and they wanted them returned. Italy could only support six clans and the seventh was unwelcome.

A clandestine meeting was hastily organized in the hinterland of the Sorrento coastal region.

"Gondo's been trespassing," said Beni. "He's not welcome on the mainland and particularly on our turf. I propose a sting operation."

"Are you in?" Dino asked the other godfathers.

They agreed without hesitation.

"Good," said Beni. I'll lay-out the details... for our eyes only, capisce?"

Each *Family* fed its informants false information, about a heist worth millions of dollars. The same information was leaked to Gondo, who found it an irresistible temptation. One clan would cause a fake disturbance as a distraction to the police. Another would block certain routes and others would back up Beni. They had informants pass on information to Gondo about where the stolen money could be intercepted. The sting was set, and we were told that he gloated insufferably about the power he'd hold over the other clans — and that he was already assuming the title of capo di tutti capi.

But Beni wanted more.

"I'm issuing a personal vendetta against Gondo," he announced before the clans departed. "His blood will be on these hands," Beni said, holding his palms up in a dramatic gesture. "This is personal... no one damages the Sorrentino family and lives."

*

After weeks of planning, the date and the location of the heist was eventually set and word was leaked to Gondo's camp. Everyone was tense those few days before, and I was concerned. Beni had ordered that no one kill Gondo... it was to be Beni alone.

At 5 a.m. on a cold November morning, Gondo's entourage crept stealthily along the inland route to Sorrento. It crept across the hilly interior above Positano, slowly and quietly navigating the blind bends.

There were four precarious bends in the road. As they swung around the fourth, Beni and Dino were waiting for them. Spotlights were spread around the hillside and beamed from every angle. There were men at the top, men at the bottom and armed men on the roadside. Gondo's cars were blindsided. Several lost control and two swerved into the trees.

Gondo's Mafiosi leapt out of their vehicles and were like rabbits, running for their lives. Our men downed each and every one of them with a barrage of bullets. Then our men pulled the only survivor out of his car and presented him to Beni. They tied his arms and legs with cord and he lay on the ground splayed out like a chicken, prepared for the barbecue.

"Gondo! You know who I am?" Beni said.

"Sure," said Gondo. His voice was shaky. "You're Beni Sorrentino."

"What else?" said Beni tormenting him.

"You're the capo di tutti..."

"That's right. So how about you show some respect?"

"Yeah, I do!"

"You're a fucking liar! You have no respect for our way of life," Beni told him, and kicked him in his side.

Gondo gasped for breath. "Beni, I'm Mafia. I'm part of the Italian *Family*!"

"You're not fit to lie on Italian soil," Beni said, and he bent down and scooped up a handful of earth. "You're scum. Say it!"

"Come on Beni..."

"Say it!"

"I'm scum!"

"You're fucking scum," Beni said again and pushed the handful of dirt into Gondo's mouth.

Gondo struggled to breathe.

"Eat it!" demanded Beni. "Eat the filthy dirt, you fucking scumbag."

Gondo coughed and struggled to swallowed it.

"You got greedy and we caught you with your hand in the cookie jar. You stole our business, trespassed on our territory… we can't allow that. The Italian Mafia stands together and you crossed us. You know our penalty for that, Gondo?"

Gondo shook his head.

Beni grabbed Gondo by his hair and lifted his head off the ground. "Look at me when I'm talking to you," he said. Then he dropped it — hard — and rested his foot on Gondo's face. "The penalty is execution at the hands of the most wronged." Beni ground his foot into Gondo's face, breaking his nose. "An eye for an eye… ever heard of that, Gondo?" Beni lifted his foot off Gondo's nose and shouted in his face. "Answer me, you fucker!"

Gondo's nose was pouring with blood and he was trembling. He looked up at Beni and answered. "Yeah Beni, I know that."

"The reason you're alive is because 'Beni the Bear' has some personal business to settle. That's me. I told the clans that I'm gonna get you… myself. You know why?"

Gondo mouthed, "No."

"You went after my family… my wife. *No one* attacks my family and lives. This is *my* vendetta," Beni said.

Gondo just stared up at Beni through his bloody face.

"It's payback time, you motherfucker and I'm your executioner."

Beni aimed his hand gun at Gondo.

"This is for the innocent women and children you murdered," he said, and shot first at Gondo's left kneecap and then at his right.

Gondo let out a scream.

"Scream all you want, no one's gonna save a lowlife fucking scumbag."

Beni then aimed at his shoulders, left and right, followed by his shins and feet.

"I'm saving the best for last," he said. "You fuck with my wife, you get this…" Beni stuck the nozzle of his gun into Gondo's groin. "I'm gonna blow your balls off."

That last bullet inflicted the most pain and Gondo was left to bleed out.

Beni stood a minute and watched him writhe in agony.

"It's all about respect," Beni told him. "You had no respect."

*

Word of Gondo's death soon travelled throughout Italy. The sting sent a powerful message to all aspiring Mafiosi with thoughts of following in Gondo's footsteps: you mess with the Families and you'll die a slow and painful death. It was recorded as the worst massacre since the infamous St Valentine's Day massacre of 1929.

I was always pleased when Beni returned safely from one of these raids. For sure, Gondo was evil and cruel, but I found the pleasure he took in the killings quite repulsive.

"You're safe now," he said to me, "this is a time for celebration. We can all sleep soundly in our beds tonight."

But he didn't return to *my* bed, that night.

*

I remember the next stage of my life vividly. It was the Spring of 1991 and I'd just turned forty-four years old. It was my favorite season. The new leaves were bright green, blossom was budding on the fruit trees and the sweet scented spring flowers burst with a profusion of color. But for me, it became the season of sadness and goodbyes.

I received an unexpected call from Mendel. Neta was in the hospital… I was on the next flight to the US.

Neta was in bad physical shape. During the past two years, her passion for desserts had caused her to become diabetic and sadly, she'd slipped into a diabetic coma. Her heart was weak and she died within hours of my arrival. I sat with Mendel at her bedside, holding both of their hands long after she'd slipped away. We cried all night.

The next day, I directed my sadness into the task of organizing her funeral ceremony; the levayah; the accompaniment of her body to her place of burial. Traditionally, Jewish funerals take place within twenty-four hours, so I worked at a fast pace.

"Mendel dear, do you have a list of people whom you wish to invite?" I asked.

"Just our local friends, Gilda," he said, handing me the names he'd sketched on note paper. "We don't have any living relatives… they're all gone now." His tone was one of great sorrow, not only for the loss of Neta, but for all the family souls who had preceded him, including his daughter.

I read the list, "Mendel, you've forgotten David," I said.

"David's gone. I'm sorry Gilda, I should have told you, but with Neta's passing…"

"Where's he gone?" I interrupted.

"We don't know. He simply disappeared. His mother told Neta that he'd left their house last week, in the middle of the night."

"I must see her," I said, as I grabbed my coat and darted out of the house.

I broke into a run as I turned the street corners, without a care for my Mafiosi. My mind was racing with terrifying scenarios of David's fate. Did the Mafia take him? Had they discovered he was FBI? Or perhaps Beni had discovered our affair? Last of all…was he alive or dead?

David's mother answered the door, "Gilda, thank God you're here," she said, throwing her arms around me. "I'm beside myself with worry."

I calmed her best I could and asked for an explanation.

"David woke me at around 3 am. last Tuesday," she began, "I will never forget his words.

'Mama, remember I told you that one day I may have to leave quickly?' he'd said. 'That time has come, Mama. I want you to be brave and not to ask questions.' And then he kissed me and was gone."

"Did he say where he was going or why?" I asked.

"No, it all happened in a matter of minutes. It seemed like a dream… but it was real," she said, as tears trickled down her cheeks. "I was never allowed to know exactly what he did… but I knew it was dangerous." She sobbed, and I held her until she was calm.

"He didn't tell you so you'd be safe," I replied. "You can't tell what you don't know. But, if anyone comes around asking questions, you let me know immediately," I said.

My inclination was that David had been tipped off that he was about to be hit and he'd gone to a safe house… but that was only a guess. I prayed that I was right.

*

"Gilda, did you ever find out what happened?" I cautiously asked.

"Yes, but my story has more sadness to tell before I deviate," she said.

*

It was a dreadful time. First Neta, then David… I didn't know what to expect. Mendel was a lost soul without Neta by his side.

"I feel as though my right arm has been ripped from my body," he said, looking distraught.

That first night without her, Mendel refused to go up to bed. He couldn't bear the thought of sleeping in their bed alone. I sat downstairs with him until his eyes closed, then I covered him with a blanket, kissed him on the forehead and went to bed. In the morning I took him some tea… but I couldn't wake him.

I touched his face and it was stone cold. Mendel had died in his sleep. I believe that he died of a broken heart.

*

"Oh Gilda!" I gasped. "How did you cope?"

"I'd had practice, Frances. Lots of practice," she replied. "Adversity marched in my shadow. Every so often it would tap me on the shoulder and when I turned around, it would stab me in the heart."

*

My task was now to arrange a joint funeral ceremony and I alone led the levayah of my parents. This was the second time I'd buried parents. Most people get to do it once, but then I'd had the joy of finding Neta and Mendel after my birth parents' tragic death.

Beni had flown to the US to support me, but when it was over and all had paid their respects, I requested time alone. He understood and left me to settle their affairs.

I set about clearing their home and placed the business up for sale. My days passed in tears and my evenings the worse for wine. I'd filled a box with cards and letters of sympathy that I'd received and which I knew would need answering. A week after the funeral I sat down with a paper-knife and began that awesome task.

One card I opened was blank. But there was a letter taped to the inside and as I read the first words, I realized that it was from David. He explained that his cover had been blown; when he'd been recognized by a field agent, who'd gone rogue. He'd been taken immediately to a safe house, until new documents had been issued, with a different identity. I understood that he could divulge neither his name nor whereabouts. I was just happy he was alive.

He expressed his sadness on hearing of Neta's and Mendel's passing and wished he could be with me. His words were affectionate and loving and I hated his absence, although I knew I'd have to accept a life without him; never to communicate or see him again. I remember the feeling of absolute loneliness. The aching we experience when part of us is missing. How loved ones can leave a vacuum in our soul… a hole in our heart and I was now riddled with holes. I didn't know how I was to recover.

*

"Gilda, you look tired… it's been an intense session," I said. "Shall we stop now?"

"Yes, Frances," Gilda agreed, "although my memories are beautiful, they're also emotionally draining. I think I'll lie down and rest for a couple of hours."

"Of course," I agreed. "I'll need a couple of hours to catch up with transcribing our recordings."

*

I stayed in New Jersey until I had a secure buyer for Mendel's and Neta's jewelry business. I'd inherited the business, some cash and all their worldly goods. I had no desire to keep the jewelry business, even with trustworthy managers in place, it would have been untenable. Every corner of the house held memories… each room echoed Neta's voice or Mendel's laugh. My room held the shadows of lovemaking in the dark when the house was quiet. This place belonged to David and me. It was our sanctuary — and now that too had gone.

My grief was raw and it was time to leave NJ for good and return to Italy. I boarded a flight to Rome and as I looked down at the Jersey shore fading into the sea, I realized that with endings come new beginnings. My recovery was in my freedom and my freedom was in Beni's best interest. I just had to convince him that it was his idea.

*

At home in Sorrento I requested that Beni and I have a serious talk.

"Beni, I need some time to grieve," I told him. "You've dealt with death, first your parents and then your uncle and other family members too. You know how it feels."

Beni reached out his hand and placed it tenderly on mine.

"You're a good man," I told him, "and now it's time for us to release each other from our obligations."

He looked confused.

"Beni, I'm forty-four years old and I'm done with NJ. I want to start a fresh phase in my life. I love you Beni, but we both know that our stormy romance has passed. You have Sophia and your children and I need to be elsewhere. It's degrading for me to walk in her shadow."

"Gilda, it is she who walks in yours! No one could replace you. You are a rock to the *Family*… and to me. I couldn't manage without you."

I leaned over and kissed him on the cheek. "Dear Beni, you and I have fulfilled our contract to one another. You kept your promise to my parents and protected them for which I'm truly grateful. I in turn kept my promise to you and was a good wife."

"You were — are — and much more… you're a Mafia queen and I love you for that. But I understand how you feel. We are friends and will remain husband and wife." He lifted his hand and shook his index finger pointedly at me. "For there is no divorce in our family." As if I could forget. "What is it you want, Gilda?" he asked.

"I want to live apart and free you to be a father," I said. "Now that Nonno has gone and you have two children."

"You want to leave Sorrento?"

"I'm grieving, Beni. I need to be elsewhere to heal. I'll visit and continue my obligation to oversee the financial accounts at the end of each tax year. But I need to occupy my mind with different work… I need a change. I want to return to the gold and diamond trade that my father taught me. I want to begin trading."

"Oh Gilda, I'll miss you," he said, looking forlorn. Beni could be so sentimental. "Where do you want to live?"

"I want to buy a small home in Geneva. It's a natural base for working and traveling around Europe," I said. "Switzerland is a country between my birth parents' lands. My father came from Austria and my mother from Italy. It's neutral territory… a country without Mafia."

"This is quite unorthodox. You know how I feel about our traditions."

"Times have changed. I'll still be part of the *Family*, I just want to recover and I can't do it here," I said, firmly. "There's too much bloodshed."

"But life without you Gilda…what if I need to talk with you?" he said.

"Then you pick up a telephone… it is 1991! And I'll visit often," I said, trying to sound convincing. "Beni, I've lived with the reality that one day you'll take a hit and you won't come home. I can't do that anymore." I pleaded, hoping he'd understand.

"Oh Gilda, this has been hard for you, I see that now. And recently so much death to contend with," he replied. "But how do I keep you safe? You're a known Mafia queen."

"Perhaps I could take a loyal soldato with me? One of the older men?" I suggested. "I intend to live modestly and I'll use Neta's and Mendel's money to buy an apartment."

"I'll buy you anything you want Gilda, just find a house and it's yours." His offer was generous and reflected his nature. "Make sure it can be secured and I'll send my best soldato to protect you."

He walked over to the safe, unlocked it and pulled out wads of cash which he placed in a large bag. "Here Gilda, open a Swiss bank account and use half to buy a house and invest the rest. It will enable you to begin trading," he said. "But then, who am I to instruct you on finances?" And he laughed.

"Thank you, dear Beni." and I kissed him. "I'm so sorry I couldn't give you children," I said.

"That was always a great sadness of mine. You'd have made a wonderful mother. The bloodline is important. I need a son to take my place."

"Or a daughter," I said, smiling.

"Yes Gilda, you have proved that a woman can do a fine job within the Mafia," and he laughed.

Our conversation was now lighter and his parting words were touching. "I wouldn't have missed these years with you for the world, Gilda." Then he kissed me one last time.

Beginnings
Day Fourteen

"Good morning Gilda," I said, sitting down beside her. "I see you're braving the green health beverage again."

"I'm following my doctor's orders," she said, "He's bullying me about staying healthy."

"Are you unwell?" I enquired.

"The body breaks down as you age, my dear. I'm supposed to ingest nutritional food, but this looks and tastes awful!"

"You're not old," I told her.

"Old enough to know that a little of what you fancy does you good… and this doesn't fit that description." She placed the green shake on one side and poured herself a large cup of coffee.

Together we indulged in our usual Viennese coffee and pastries. Fifteen minutes later, we were fit to begin our day.

*

I was excited at the prospect of working for myself in a business that I knew from my youth. I embraced the opportunity to study the gold and diamond markets again and acquire the knowledge I needed for present-day trading. I had much to learn.

I remained in Sorrento for a year. Beni had granted me permission to leave, but he'd insisted on two conditions. The first was that I must successfully train and supervise the handover of our financial affairs, for which I recruited two accountants known to the *Family*. They were to manage the day-to-day running of the finances, but I also recruited an astute consigliere who would keep a shrewd eye out for any fraudulent behavior. The Mafia dealt mainly in cash, to avoid paying taxes and to cover their covert deals. But our accounts had to show *some* evidence of legitimate business, to protect our network of politicians, who turned a blind eye for a tidy fee.

The second condition was that I should never take a lover. I would remain married to him and in return he'd protect me.

*

"Oh Gilda," I said, "that's a life sentence."

"Yes Frances, a life without love for as long as Beni was alive," she replied.

"Was it worth it?" I asked. "You were only forty-four."

"Unequivocally, yes. I had to get away, just like you Frances, except my escape was more difficult. I was totally dependent on Beni's acquiescence and his kind heart. I gladly accepted his conditions. Remember, I'd experienced a great love in my life... I was luckier than most," she said, smiling gently.

*

In 1992, I traveled to Geneva in search of a new home. Beni had given me enough money to purchase a comfortable house, but I decided only to spend a quarter of the cash on a home. I spent days searching property in and around Geneva, until I discovered the town of Carouge. It sat on the outskirts of Geneva and was originally built by Italian architects. I knew instantly that it was where I would make my home. A house had just become vacant, overlooking the Place du Marche, where twice a week they held a fresh produce market. It was a perfect size for me, so I decorated, bought furniture and moved in within a month. I lived there happily for six years.

My soldato, Mario, occupied rooms on the ground floor, where he could intercept any intruder. An unlikely occurrence for most people, but for the wife of a godfather he was a necessary fixture. I knew that I would always be tied to the Mafia... it's an institution one can never truly leave. I also feared that if Beni died, I would never get out. Beni was nicknamed "Beni the Bear" for good reason; he was large and had a kind heart... Dino was not so kind. I was aware that the twins did not share that gene and I'd often thought that if I were to be kidnapped, Beni would pay the ransom... Dino would not.

*

After I'd bought the house, I invested the money which I'd inherited from Neta and Mendel,'s estate and deposited a portion of the cash Beni had given me, into a Swiss bank account, leaving myself a substantial sum on which to live and trade. I also placed some cash inside my home safe, in case I needed to flee. I was still married to the godfather of the Sorrentino clan. I had a price on my head. There were bounty-hunters and rogue Mafiosi who were capable of kidnapping me in exchange for money and although I was vigilant and well trained, I was never complacent.

*

The gold and diamond industries are cult-like. You need connections to trade. These industries are tight and impenetrable unless you have family or friends in the business. The traders will turn you away if you're an unknown, but luckily I *was* known. It had been eighteen years since I last watched and learned from my father and I was out of touch. But, like riding a bike… once learned, you never forget.

I began by applying the first principle of business; to connect with known sources. So I prepared for a trip to Amsterdam.

*

The flight from Geneva was short and with my soldato behind the wheel of the rental car, we entered the town of my youth. I was overcome with a flush of emotion and through glazed eyes I surveyed every corner, every house. I swung my head from side to side, dizzily searching for a familiar face. In the main street we stopped directly outside my parents' old jewelry business. I sat quite still for a while and felt a surge of anger rising from within.

"They're not here," I murmured out loud.

"Signora? Cosa hai detto?" Mario said.

"My parents, they should be…"

My emotions had been triggered by the sight of the building and I'd regressed years in an instant.

"Stai bene, signora?" Mario seemed concerned.

"I'm okay… si, sto bene, grazie."

I'd loved and lost and loved again. I'd had two sets of wonderful parents. I'd emigrated twice and experienced many unpredictable events and I still had much to achieve. I had to be strong and endure the pain of revisiting my past.

I climbed out of the car, walked towards the shop front and pushed the security button. An older man looked at me, decided I was not a risk and buzzed me inside.

"Goedemorgen," I said, and as I approached him, the expression on his face began to change.

"I can't believe it!" he said. "Rulah, come… come here quick."

A woman in her sixties came running from the back room. "O Jee!" she said. "Gilda, is it you?"

They hugged me so tight that I thought I'd burst, then they closed the shop and we talked. They'd heard about the crash, which caused the tragic death of my parents, but they didn't know what had happened to me. I shared part of my story; I recounted my years in NJ and Italy, but I omitted my connection with the Mafia.

"I want to get back into trading again, but I've lost all my parents' connections," I told them.

"We managed to buy your parents' old business after your emigrated," Rulah said. "It's been hugely profitable and now…" tears began to cascade down her cheeks. "Excuse me Gilda, but I'm quite overcome with emotion."

"What she wants to say, is that we'd be pleased to help you. We could introduce you to the best in the business."

"And reconnect you with your parents' friends."

"I'd really appreciate that, but first I'd like to take you to dinner," I said.

"And will you stay the night, Gilda?" offered Rulah.

"Thank you, that's a generous offer, but I've already booked a hotel," I said.

Hal looked outside and noticed the car with my soldato in the driver's seat. "Is he with you?" he asked.

"Ah… yes," I said. I hadn't prepared how I would explain a bodyguard, so I fumbled a quick reply. "He's my driver."

"You must have done well for yourself Gilda," he said sizing up the situation. "You have money to invest?"

"I do, and I intend to work hard and double it!" They laughed and nodded their heads in agreement.

During the next week I was introduced to all who mattered. They were a mixture of new and old faces in the gold and diamond business. Most of all I enjoyed meeting my parents' friends again, as Rulah took me around the town. My only sadness was that Gina and Hans had passed away.

"What's happened to all the synagogues?" I asked. "There used to be five, beautiful, lively…"

"They're gone. Four remained empty for years and were eventually sold to the city," Rulah said.

"Why?"

"Because my dear, they could no longer fill them. Only a few out of the seventy-nine thousand, four hundred and ten Jews, who lived in Amsterdam survived the Holocaust and came home. "

"Oh Rulah, you know the exact number—"

"Of course… we can never forget.

"Others, like your parents and us, managed to stay alive by deceiving the Germans into thinking we were Dutch Protestants and Catholics," she painfully explained.

"Forgive me, It's been a long time. I didn't think before I spoke," I said.

"You were born after the war and you were only seventeen when you left. For us, everywhere holds a memory. Every day we see faces of lost loved ones reflected in every building, on every corner of every street. It's still raw… we never forget," she said again.

I felt ashamed that I asked such an insensitive question. But Rulah read my mind. "We lucky ones have a future and we're going to help you build yours," she said, altering her tone to one more uplifting.

*

By the time I returned to Geneva, I'd accumulated a list of trading contacts and the knowledge to trade in the present gold and diamond markets. Their warm welcome had rekindled my trust in mankind and it felt good to be alive and working again. Now I was ostensibly single again, I chose to revert to my original Dutch maiden name, Karter. When my parents and I had entered the US, our name was anglicized to Carter by the immigration officers.

After six months of trading I was making money. Each year I exceeded my annual profits and on the fifth year anniversary of my business, I'd accrued enough to fulfil two promises I'd made to myself many years before.

*

"Gilda, I think I know what one of your promises was, now that you were living feely in Geneva," I suggested. "Was it to reconnect with David?"

"Sadly no, my dear. David and I accepted that we could never be together again… not even in Geneva. The risk was too great. Remember, David's cover had been blown and it would have been easy for the Mafia to connect the dots and realize that I was a co-conspirator against racketeering in NJ. I'd played my part by inciting the gangs to turn against each other and I'd informed on our faction. To this day, they assume I knew nothing," she explained.

"I understand the risks, All the same, it seems so unfair, Beni had his lovers."

"Frances, it didn't work that way in Italy."

"But you weren't *in* Italy!"

"It didn't work that way in any place, because I was still legally married to an Italian godfather! My dear girl, in those days within the Mafia there was one rule for the men and another for us women. David and I had something very special. Something most people only dream of and we were grateful for that. We couldn't take the risk of being together again, we'd have been killed if discovered."

"I'm so sad for you Gilda," I said.

"Don't be," Gilda replied, smiling gently. "We survived. We pushed reality away until its inevitable arrival, by living in the moment," she said. "Remember, Frances, that passion is the driver in life. Either for ambition or love and sometimes… revenge."

"So, what were those promises?" I asked.

"All will become clear after lunch," Gilda said.

*

After we had eaten, just before Gilda and I continued with her story, the housekeeper entered the room.

"Frances, this arrived for you," she said, handing me a large padded envelope. I was surprised and looked at the return address. It was from my sister, Mary.

"Frances, is everything alright?" Gilda asked, noticing the perplexed expression on my face.

"I'm not sure," I replied. "I don't remember giving her this address." I put the envelope aside to open later, but it played on my mind throughout the afternoon.

*

The year was 1997 and I'd just turned fifty years old. I couldn't believe how I'd turned my life around. Perhaps it was the spirit of my father directing me to the wealthiest buyers, or just my persistent nature that led me to succeed. I know that I worked diligently to acquire my own wealth which I needed in order to fulfill my promises.

That first promise had been festering inside me for thirty years. Each year, I'd postpone the task by convincing myself that I needed more money to devise and implement the perfect plan.

I was prompted by an accidental encounter at Geneva International Airport. For as we both know, there are no accidents in life. I was returning from Amsterdam and for some reason I looked across at the other gate, where people were waiting to board a flight to Los Angeles. There was a man walking to join the passenger boarding line. Suddenly, he turned and looked in my direction and we locked eyes. Our moment of joint recognition was together startling and deathly cold. Then, emotion began to kick in and my heart began pounding.

If it weren't for the glass panel that divided us, I'm not sure what would have happened. Perhaps I'd have lashed out? He didn't linger, and I watched as he pushed his way through the crowd to escape my hatred. For that was the look on my face... sheer and utter hatred.

This was the man who'd abused me and left me for dead! He'd destroyed my chance of having more children. He'd lied and he'd stolen my inheritance. He was a thief, a fraud and an abuser and I'd vowed, many years before, that one day I'd find Michael Allen and kill him. And there he was... a few feet beyond my reach. An intense feeling of violent revenge consumed me, as if it had all happened yesterday. I swear I heard Eli's voice in my head, spurring me on to victory.

The following week the newspaper ran an article about a young woman, which terrified me. It stated that Heidi Farve, from Geneva, Switzerland, had been studying languages in California at a private college, where she met American-born Professor Michael Allen. They became close friends and he accompanied Heidi to her home in Geneva. She alleged that, after attending a private dinner last Saturday, Professor Allen became very drunk and abused her, beating and kicking her until she passed out.

The young woman who shared Heidi's apartment, returned on Sunday morning to find her lying on the floor, unconscious and bloody. She immediately called the emergency services. Police were trying to locate Professor Allen.

*

"Frances, I was so shocked. I couldn't calm down. I'd seen him... there at the airport the previous Sunday morning. If I'd known then that he'd abused this beautiful girl..." Gilda was terribly upset as she relived this moment of pain.

"But you didn't know," I said, trying to calm her again.

"Yes but, if I'd acted sooner and fulfilled my vow to kill him, none of this would have happened," she said, holding her hands over her face as if to hide her shame.

"Gilda, you're talking about *killing* a man? This is no small deed…"

"There are those we encounter in our lives who we say we'd like to kill, due to some dispute or other. And there are those who really *deserve* to die, for committing evil atrocities. Seldom do we follow through with action, but I always vowed I would. After reading that news report of the attack, I knew I had to hunt him down… it was a decisive moment."

I'd never seen Gilda so serious.

*

The next day I went to see the student at the hospital.

"Are you a relative?" the nurse asked.

"Yes, I'm Heidi's aunt," I lied.

The nurse escorted me to the door of the private room where this poor girl was lying. I knew that Heidi wouldn't know me, so just before she pushed open the door, I caused a diversion.

"I need a moment to compose myself," I told the nurse and took several deep breaths to emphasize my distress.

"I understand," the nurse said. "You can sit here, outside, until you feel ready," she said, directing me to a chair.

I thanked her and waited before I made my entrance. When all was quiet, I ventured inside Heidi's room and crept up to her bedside. She seemed to be sleeping, so I took the liberty of standing near and focusing on her injuries.

Her swollen face was bruised across her nose and eyes. One wrist was in plaster and her ribs were bound in bandages. I wondered if there was lasting internal damage, similar to mine. I dared not think that perhaps this beautiful young woman may be prevented from having children, too.

Suddenly, she opened her eyes.

"Who are you?" she said.

"I'm Gilda, I've come to share my story with you… if you'll listen?" I asked.

She looked puzzled. "Do I know you?" Her words were formed slowly and deliberately, as if her whole body struggled with the task.

"No, my dear, you don't know me, but we have much in common. Many years ago, when I was about your age, I too was brutally abused by Michael Allen," I told her.

Her eyes widened and her hand reached slowly for mine. I gently clasped it as a tear trickled down her cheek. We had bonded in our adversity. I sat beside her and relayed my agonizing memory of being thrown through a window from the second story of my town house, then left for dead. I listened as she painfully recalled her tragedy, too.

"Michael was my professor at uni. When I first met him I was captivated by his charisma and attentiveness. He seemed kind and despite our huge age difference, I really thought we had something special. That's when I asked him to travel with me and meet my family, here in Geneva."

"I remember how his charisma deceived me too," I said.

Heidi was unable to move her neck, but her eyes communicated agreement as she fought back the tears once again. "We'd flown overnight from Los Angeles to Geneva and rested during the day in my apartment. Later, we headed out for dinner and some bars around the town. Michael drank heavily, more than I'd ever seen him drink before. His attitude was belligerent and he was rude to my friends, so I insisted we leave. I ordered a taxi home and once we stepped inside my apartment he started pushing me and then twisting my wrist until it snapped. I yelled for him to stop… the pain was excruciating, but he said I was just another rich kid and began hitting me around the head. I fell and I remember him kicking me… I'm not sure quite what happened next, I think I was near passing out. Everything became blurry, but I remember seeing him turn my purse upside down… and that was the last time I saw him. After that, I must have passed out. The police say he stole all my credit cards and managed to use one of them to buy his flight to LA."

"My dear girl, it breaks my heart to know how you've suffered. I do hope the police find him." I said.

"My father's engaged a lawyer."

Heidi's father entered the room and gently kissed his daughter. We were introduced and I admitted that I told the staff I was a relative. Heidi briefly explained and her father requested that we talk after his visit.

I took my leave and left father and daughter alone to talk and heal. I'd offered emotional support and promised to visit again. But that was not all I had to offer.

Eagan, Heidi's father, joined me in the café by the entrance of the hospital. "The police will pursue him and prosecute," he said forcefully. "How could a grown man behave like this?"

I registered the pain in this father's eyes and felt that if my own father had lived, he too would have felt this terrible anguish. He too would have felt helpless and be searching for answers as to why a man would willfully damage a young woman in her prime.

"He's a sociopath," I told him. "I tried to prosecute, but there were no witnesses and another woman provided a false alibi." I filled him in on the gory details of my attack and long recovery.

"So, he stole everything you had?"

"Yes, everything I had, that was left to me by my parents after their accidental death."

"I'm so deeply sorry and I thank you for reaching out to us. However, I'm not sure how you can help."

"I can help, as long as you don't ask me how," I told him.

"Then I won't." His words were sincere and he held out his hand to secure the promise. "I'm pleased to have you in our lives, Gilda."

"This is my address and telephone number," I said handing him my card. "Feel free to contact me, anytime."

At home that evening, I began to devise a plan to track down Michael Allen.

*

"The next stage of my story is very detailed, so let's stop for today, Frances," Gilda said.

"Yes, of course," I said. "Please excuse me Gilda, but I need to open the package from my sister. It's been preying on my mind."

*

News from my sister was not always welcome and I feared I was in for another surprise. Once inside my room, I peeled back the flap on the padded envelope with apprehension, dreading what I may find. I took a deep breath and read her letter.

Dear Frances,

You will be surprised to learn that I've written a book. I realize that I'm a mere novice compared with you, the famous author. So it's with some trepidation that I'm sending you my manuscript for review.

It's an account of a macabre episode in my life and I warn you, it will be emotionally challenging: as the raw facts I lay before you will chill you to the bone.

I shuddered at the thought of what I would encounter within her manuscript.

There was a PS.... *For your eyes only*. So I'm not to show anyone, I thought. But why write it, if it's not meant to be read?

I picked up the wad of tightly bound paper and read the title, *The Judas Tree,* complete at 64,000 words. So she really has written a novel, I thought. Was she competing with me?

I was intrigued and my curiosity prompted me to delve into the pages and discover whatever grim facts, truths or lies I'd discover within.

I read the first page... it was alarming! I read on and on, past my dinner time and late into the night until I finished the manuscript. What little sleep I had, was periodically interrupted with excerpts from Mary's novel. Finally, at 6:30 a.m. I could no longer contain the urge to contact her. I couldn't face speaking, so I sent a text message instead.

*

Text from FRANCES: *"Mary, I've read your manuscript and although it's captivating, I found it totally unrealistic... even to one who writes fiction. I doubt any woman would go to these extremes to exercise revenge. I always knew you had a dark side, but a story has to be believable. "*

I felt it my duty to honestly critique her manuscript, knowing that she would probably push back.

*

Text from MARY: *"Unrealistic? How so? We've both suffered abuse?"*

*

Text from FRANCES: *"True, but the storyline's implausible."* I was brutal, but honest.

*

Text from MARY: *"Don't you know that fact can be stranger than fiction."*

*

Text from FRANCES: *"Yes, but this doesn't have the ring of truth about it... so where did you get the idea?"* I was trying to soften my tone.

*

Text from MARY: *"I had a village to observe and time to kill."*

*

Text from FRANCES: *"Ha-ha! Not literally, I hope?"* I joked, again to keep the conversation light.

*

Text from MARY: "*You're the fiction writer.*"

*

Text from FRANCES: I was momentarily stunned by her reply and paused to think. "*Are you saying that your story is not fiction?*"

*

Text from MARY: "*We were brought up to tell the truth and I would never lie to you.*"

*

Text from FRANCES: "*You can't be serious—*" I waited for her to confirm the joke or offer some other explanation. But there was no rebuff and her silence was deafening. "*Oh my God. Mary, what have you done?*"

*

Text from MARY: "*What have I done? How could you ask me that? How could you not understand that my actions were virtuous.*"

*

I read her text and visibly began to shake. Virtuous? She had killed a man… and she claimed that was virtuous!

*

Text from MARY: "*Frances, I can trust you… can't I?*"

*

She tells me a horrific truth and asks me to trust her? I threw my phone across the room in disgust. Anger rose within me and I felt sick. I had no choice but to live with her dirty little secret. Those vivid scenes she'd described were now forever engraved on my mind.

Aargh! I wrapped my arms around my body in an attempt to self-comfort and crashed onto my bed. I'm not sure why, but I read the text messages again. Perhaps it was to obtain a different truth in the hope of discovering something misconstrued. But this time it seemed worse, particularly when I realized her expectation of my praise.

Oh my God, she'd enveloped herself in a circle of evil and as with all circles, there was no exit.

Shared Secrets
Day Fifteen

At 7 a.m. Estela knocked on my bedroom door.

"Good morning Frances, I heard you were up," she said, handing me a small tray of juice and coffee. "Are you well?" she enquired, "you missed dinner."

"Yes, I'm fine, thank you," I politely replied. "I was very tired last night and went to sleep early. Tell Gilda I'll be down soon."

*

"Good morning Gilda, I apologize for not joining you at dinner, but I was tired... actually, I couldn't face dinner, after I'd read my sister's letter."

"Not bad news, I hope?" Gilda asked.

I looked at her and made an instant decision. "Yes, the news was awful."

"Oh my dear, I'm so sorry. Would you like to talk about it?"

"I'm not supposed to tell anyone... but you and I have shared so much, I know I can trust you... oh, but where to begin?" I said, anxiously.

"At the beginning," she replied, guiding me to the couch. "And remember, my dear, you can trust me with your life."

I sat next to her and began to unload my burden. "My sister's written a novel, the package was her manuscript. The story describes a horrific scene of torture and ultimately murder," I said, watching for her reaction.

"Go on, my dear," Gilda said, squeezing my hand.

"Well the thing is..." and then I just blurted it out, "my sister's a murderer!"

"Oh dear," she said, "that's an unfortunate burden for you to bear, particularly today."

I was confused. "Why today?" I asked.

"You see my dear... I too, am a murderer. That is *my* secret," she confessed.

I looked at her and gasped. "You were going to tell me that today?" I said.

"Yes, my dear, I'd already told you that I vowed to kill Michael Allen. Today, I'll explain just how I did it. You'll have all the details for our story," she said.

"But Gilda, if I write it, then everyone will know and you'll be arrested!" I was horrified.

"Trust me, I'll be fine," she said. "You and I are good at keeping secrets. And when the time is right, we'll publish. As for your sister, we'll keep her secret, too."

"I know my sister, she'll try and publish her novel under the guise of fiction. But if the police detective, who's been interrogating her, reads the novel… well, it will be obvious she's the murderer. How do I stop her?"

"People who commit crime usually want to be discovered," Gilda said. "Just like me. That's why I'm revealing all these atrocities."

"But it was the Mafia and others who committed the crimes you describe, Gilda," I said.

"It was me, too. I'm a murderer, or perhaps it should be, murderess?" she said.

"Gilda! How can you treat this so lightly?" I was astounded by her complacency.

"Your sister is the keeper of her secret. That she has shared it once should tell you that she's expecting a reaction. If that's not to her liking, then she'll share her story again, with someone else, and there's nothing you can do to protect her. It's human nature to seek praise and approval or to confess and seek punishment. She will decide, not you or I. All we can do is keep silent." Gilda's words were brutal, but profound.

"I can't understand how she could commit such a violent act," I said.

"If it were a crime of passion, then someone must have hurt her… she is damaged, like me. Although the man she killed may not have had the greatest impact on her life, he may have pushed her to the edge of the precipice from which there is no escape."

I listened carefully and tried hard to understand her reasoning.

"Now that we've shared our deepest secrets, do you feel relieved?" Gilda asked.

"I do, but I can only cope with one murderer today, so I'll place the other in a drawer until some future date," I told her. And with all my willpower I smiled, and we began this extraordinary work day.

*

This revelation is about a score I had to settle, and so I began a clandestine search for Michael Allen. It was a personal vendetta... a task I had to perform alone without involving the *Family*, as I could never risk Beni discovering that I'd had a son. But for my own physical safety, I decided that Mario and one other trusted Mafioso would accompany me.

I hired a private investigator, who narrowed the search to the Los Angeles area of California, which fitted with Heidi's story. The PI managed to trace Michael's movements through various positions he'd held at universities. He discovered a history of accusations and unproven cases of assault levelled against this man, including multiple restraining orders. The police records showed that he'd become more criminally minded, targeting young female students from wealthy families and extorting money from them. But the PI couldn't find him. Michael had the cunning of a fox and could disappear down a fox-hole when he detected someone on his trail.

For three weeks, my PI searched for some clue to his whereabouts. But LA is a huge place and Michael had gone to ground. It was then that a miracle occurred. I received a letter. It had no return address label, but it did have a postmark on the envelope. It was mailed in Anchorage, Alaska.

My darling,

Although we're apart, we are never truly separate. I keep a watchful eye on your life from afar and my vigilance had brought news of Michael Allen's crimes. I anticipated your actions and discovered some information. This evil man is living at a friend's apartment, while it is vacant. He dare not apply to a university in CA so act quickly before he moves States again. The address is below. I have a secure contact in LA. His name is Billy and he will lend you an untraceable SUV with black tinted windows. Use it only for the hit... but then, my dear, who am I to tell a Mafia queen how to proceed?

I know you and you know me... we are as one mind, one heart. You must do what you always intended, especially now. Take care my love.

Loving you always and forever,

David.

I burned his letter, after I learned it by heart. I knew to destroy incriminating evidence... there was no need for David to instruct me... he knew that I would. I slept easier that night, knowing that at least one person I loved was safe and maybe reachable, sometime, someday.

*

Now that I had an address and Billy's number I moved to implement stage two of my plan, and I told no one.

I found a clinic in Switzerland whose innovative methods were just within the bounds of the law. I wanted to know if it were possible to erase memories of abuse. I'd previously researched this topic and believed that it was. I was told that a solution was possible and it involved taking some prescribed drugs, which cost a small fortune... but they were worth every franc. The clinic and I drew up a contract, which was signed by two doctors and myself. It stipulated absolute discretion from all parties.

*

"Frances, I don't want to divulge the name of the clinic... you understand?" Gilda said.

"Of course," I replied, wondering what other incredible facts I'd learn today.

*

I began by consulting one of their psychiatrists about the traumatic assault I suffered at the hand of Michael Allen. Time was of the essence, so I made special arrangements to speed up the consultation. First, I had to commit to a brain scan and then a preliminary procedure.

The doctors began by boring a small hole in my skull, which they numbed for entry, but unbelievably the rest of the procedure was quite painless. Then, the brain surgeons skilfully inserted a probe through my skull and began testing the reactions of certain synaptic connections, with an electromagnetic wand. I remained conscious for this exploration into my traumatic past. My input was a vital part of their discovery. When we identified the area, I felt the same emotional surge of panic that I'd experienced during the assault. Although it was not a physical reality, it was quite terrible to relive that incident.

*

"Frances, I need some water. The stress is making my mouth dry," she said.

"Of course," I said and fetched a glass. I sat holding her hand until she composed herself. "I don't know how you've managed to cope with these events Gilda."

She just squeezed my hand and smiled. After a moment, we resumed.

*

The neurotransmitter associated with the memory lit up on the computer screen. The neuro-surgeons then targeted it with a specific chemical. It was in preparation for the drugs I'd ingest at a later date, which would interact with the chemical and erase my traumatic memory. This procedure was still in the experimental stage of development and carried a risk. The medical term is oxigenetics — it's a way of manipulating memory.

These Swiss neuroscientists had created a ground-breaking procedure. Before this scientific discovery, they performed simple experiments with propranolol which blocked norepinephrine after recall and therefore blocked memory. But these drugs often caused false memories, which were dangerous. The patient wouldn't know which memories were real; false memories can be just as painful and extremely damaging. Also, these changes were not encoded, which means they were not set for life and flashbacks would occur, in time. I sought a more advanced method. But like all experimental medicine, it carried a risk… one I was prepared to take.

*

"Frances, it's been an emotional morning, let's break here for something to eat," Gilda said.

Lunch was a welcome hiatus from this clinical description.

*

Now that I had an address for Michael Allen, I planned a trip to LA to surprise him. I was accompanied by my two trusted Mafiosi; Mario and his brother Sergio, whom I knew would guard and support me in my mission. I sent Sergio ahead to organize a rental car in which to meet us. We landed in LA late at night, after a direct daytime flight. We immediately drew the attention of what we called the Mickey Mouse clan — the LA Mafia. I knew we'd be watched, not only by them, but also by the CIA.

A man in plain clothes addressed me. "Signora Sorrentino," he said. He was flanked by a customs officer. I didn't answer, so he tried again. "Excuse me, signora," he said, standing in my path.

"Yes," I said. "What is it."

'Signora Sorrentino…"

"That's not my name. It's Gilda Karter." I corrected him and showed him my passport. He smirked and then asked me why I was visiting LA.

"I'm here on business," I told him and handed him my card.

"So, you're in the gold and diamond industry now," he said. "We're well aware who you are."

"Obviously not, as you addressed me by the wrong name. Now, I'm tired after my flight and I'd like to get to my hotel," I said. I knew he had nothing on me, it was simply my association with the Mafia and for sure, the Mickey Mouse clan had tipped them off. The last thing they wanted was visiting Mafia from other clans trespassing on their territory.

He stood aside and Mario and I walked to our waiting car. As we sped to our hotel, I noticed we had a tail.

"Do you want me to lose them?" Sergio asked.

"No need to draw attention today. Tomorrow we may have to outrun them," I told him and relaxed into the seat.

I had a suite with adjoining rooms for the men. There was always the threat of an abduction from the hotel when we traveled. We'd told no one the location of the hotel, so I was surprised by a telephone call.

"Gilda, I'm concerned. Why are you in LA? It's not safe for you." It was Beni's voice.

"Ciao Beni, I'm fine. I'm here on business... my business. Don't worry, I have Mario and Sergio with me." He was kind to call, but it was a sharp reminder of just how fast news travelled through Mafia channels.

*

The next day we took a ride to Santa Monica, ostensibly for me to enjoy a little shopping. After we'd played the game, we drove around and found the apartment block where Michael was holed up. I had a clear view through the tinted car windows without evoking suspicion. We dropped Mario off a block from the apartment, so he could plan our evening visit. He returned with a photographed agenda which we studied. We mentally rehearsed our tactical maneuvers and returned to the hotel.

At 7 p.m. Sergio and I left the hotel in the rental car, followed by the CIA. We were en route to attend a private party in a client's mansion, off Sunset Boulevard. This was to be the business trip focus, and my cover. It was by invitation only which we waved at the guard on the security gate and joined the long line of cars and limos extending along the driveway.

Our CIA friends were not so lucky. They were held at the gate, pending verification.

Once we reached the main entrance, I joined the flow of guests and Sergio proceeded to the private valet parking area. We were aware that the CIA was watching our every move, but now it was from a distance... which assisted our plan.

I mingled for an hour and made certain I was noticed. Then at 8:30 p.m. I discreetly walked to a side entrance and waited in the shadows until Mario arrived in the black SUV on loan from Billy. As arranged, he'd told the security guard that he'd been called to collect his client earlier than planned. I slipped into the SUV and behind the black tinted windows, I changed my shoes and pulled on a dark functional jacket to hide my cocktail wear.

Further along the driveway we paused momentarily for Sergio to join us. Our trio was complete and we departed incognito, without the CIA on our tail.

We drove to Santa Monica and parked outside the rear entrance of the apartment block we'd surveyed earlier that day. My heart was pounding in my chest. I think it was partly the realization that the moment of reckoning had arrived — and the fact that I'd never killed anyone before.

My two Mafiosi stealthily climbed the stone stairs to the eighth floor, and listened outside the door of apartment 812. The television was on when they slipped the lock and entered unheard by the occupant.

Michael was sitting in an armchair as the two Mafiosi grabbed him from behind. Mario grabbed his throat while Sergio bound his body to the chair with cable wire. Then they wrapped the remaining cable wire around his throat, leaving two feet hanging, like a leash. I waited five minutes and then proceeded with the next part of our plan.

I climbed the stairs to the eighth floor... it was quite a hike, but it was essential that we were not seen on CCTV cameras. Sergio was standing with the front door ajar. I took a deep breath and entered the apartment. I nodded to Mario, who swung Michael around in his chair and I stood before him... as judge and jury.

"What the hell?" He looked stunned.

"Hello Michael," I said. "I bet you never thought you'd meet me again. Although, you looked shocked to see me at the airport in Geneva. I know why you were there... you were on the run, again. You'd beaten that poor student Heidi to a pulp and left her for dead. That seems to be a habit of yours."

"What d'ya want Gilda? Money? I don't have any," he said.

"I'm a wealthy woman, I have lots of money. No, sadly for you, that's not why I'm here."

"Then get the fuck out…" he began to shout. Sergio immediately turned up the TV volume and placed duct tape across Michael's mouth.

"I've been waiting a long time for this moment," I said. "Give me a few minutes alone with this lowlife, would you?" I said to the men.

"Sure Gilda, we'll be the other side of that door, okay?" said Mario.

I pulled up a hard-backed chair and sat opposite Michael. "Do you think after all these years I'm going to walk away just because you tell me?" and I laughed. "I'm not going to make this easy for you… you see, today is a day of reckoning. Today, I'm seeking retribution for what you did to me all those years ago.

"What punishment befits a person so wicked as to cruelly punish a woman for carrying his child, then leave her for dead? How should I calculate that sinful deed? Personally, I believe in the Jewish law … an eye for an eye and a tooth for a tooth.

"But let me list the evil acts you've committed and then I'll decide the punishment.

"Firstly, you walked away from your son and left me without support. You stole all my money. You fraudulently took my home and my inheritance. You harmed the woman carrying your own child and then you took from me my chance of having more children. You destroyed my health and caused me years of physical pain. But worst of all, you pushed me through a glass pane, from the second story of a building, and left me for dead. The only good thing is that after today, no women will suffer at your evil hands. You will be gone. But first, you will suffer as I and countless other women have suffered. You will feel pain that is so excruciating, you'll wish you were dead."

I stopped to breathe and turned away from him; I could no longer bear to look at his face. Then I opened the door and called the men back into the room. "Let's do it," I said.

Mario and Sergio cut Michael loose from the chair, but kept his feet bound and his hands tied behind his back. I switched off the lights as they dragged him outside to the balcony, where they stood him with his back against the rail. They gave me the leash, which was attached to his neck. I pulled it just tight enough to cause panic… but not enough to strangle him.

"Feeling frightened now, are you?" I asked. "I could kill you with this cable, but that's too easy. No, you're going to fly through the air, as I did… but your flight will be from the eighth story and you are going to land on hard concrete. Turn him around so he can see," I told the men. "Can you anticipate the pain? No? Okay Mario, hit his knees."

Mario took a hammer out of his jacket and smashed it against each knee in turn. Michael began to crumble in pain.

"Hold him up, so his weight presses on his knees… he needs a lesson in pain," I instructed them. "Now, let's go for the hands," I said.

They released one hand at a time and smashed it with the hammer, shattering all the bones. "You won't be using *those* again to beat and abuse women. Or to steal their money, their lives and the lives of their unborn children."

He hung limply between my two Mafiosi and at last I felt satisfaction at seeing him suffer. "It's time," I said. "After all these years I've waited for this moment of revenge and it is *sweet*."

The men untied Michael, all the while keeping him upright and steady against the rail. Lastly, they removed the cable from around his throat and ripped off the duct tape. They quickly checked around and when all was clear they nodded to me.

This was the sign… the moment I'd waited for. I looked him in the eyes, so he would remember the image of hatred as his last memory on this earth. Then, I took his feet and hurled him backwards over the rail.

He hit the ground with a thud and splattered his blood across white concrete slabs, turning them red. The sight of his blood on white brought back memories of my own body bleeding into the snow and Eli's words. 'The punishment must fit the crime', he'd told me.

"It's done Eli." I was muttering out loud.

"Gilda, are you okay?" Mario asked, as he gently touched my shoulder. "We have to go… now!"

We closed up the apartment and hurried down the stairs. Sergio drove the car around a couple of blocks before driving past the front of the apartment building. A crowd was gathering around Michael's body. We drove slowly on, through the town and back to the party.

Once we reached the security gate, Sergio showed the guard the invitation again and we entered without CIA interference, due to the black tinted windows and the fact they assumed I was still partying.

I reassembled my cocktail outfit and entered the house once again.

Mario drove the car out after depositing Sergio to the valet parking area. All had gone like clockwork. I headed directly to the bar and downed a double vodka. At 11 p.m. Sergio brought the rental car to the main entrance and collected me. We drove out of the gates, followed by the CIA, who unwittingly gave me a solid alibi.

*

The next morning I enjoyed breakfast in bed while watching the news on TV. The fatal fall from the Santa Monica apartment was reported as a probable suicide. Michael Allen had a string of accusations and fraud cases pending at his time of death. The news also stated that the Swiss police had a warrant for his arrest, which now would be redundant.

I sat back and heaved a sigh of relief.

*

Once home and ensconced in the privacy of my house in Carouge, I updated my journal which I wrote daily and added a true and detailed account of my trip to LA, describing the killing of Michael Allen. The purpose of this documentation, was for my biography. I then visited my bank and dropped the journal into my safe deposit box.

My next chore was to write an account of my trip to LA, omitting the killing and any contact with Michael Allen. This account of events would be the one which I would learn after I had erased my memory. It was basically my insurance against the drugs malfunctioning.

*

"Gilda, I'm confused. You say that you consulted the clinic because you needed to erase the memory of the assault and abuse by Michael Allen," I asked. "But I thought you needed to erase the memory of your killing Michael in Santa Monica?"

"That's correct. You're very astute, Frances. But I could hardly have walked into the clinic and announce that I planned to commit murder! But that was exactly the case. Let me continue with the story, so that you understand," Gilda said.

*

The neuro-surgeons at the clinic had been explicit when they told me that I'd lose all memory which was emotionally associated with Michael. They had to be assured that I understood the implications. Of course, they were unaware that this was precisely what I wanted and *why* I planned the murder to mirror the assault he'd inflicted on me. The emotional connection I'd forged by creating similar circumstances for my revenge killing, would be triggered by the original memory of the assault, and would also be wiped out.

*

"An eye for an eye... now I understand why you followed this rule," I said.

Gilda gave me a wry smile before she answered.

"Remember, my dear, that Eli was my mentor. Through his strength I found the will to live so that one day I could take my revenge. Eli learnt the Jewish law about retribution from the Torah, which consists of the first five books of the Old Testament. The books of Exodus, Leviticus and Deuteronomy all state the law of an eye for an eye... but its origins derive from the preceding Babylonian law, where it is written that a person (or their relative) who belongs to a group, such as the Mafia, which abides by its own laws, has the right to seek retribution on the person who caused them an injury. And that they can inflict a punishment *worse* than the original crime. I'm still a Mafia queen, I followed Mafia law, I mirrored the crime and chose the punishment. I chose death.

"Don't be shocked, my dear. Those who commit evil acts should be punished harshly and compassion saved for the deserving," Gilda said.

I acknowledged her words and she continued.

*

I did have reservations about the drugs. I was fearful they would wipe out more than my traumatic memories. As insurance, I wrote the passcode for the deposit box and other vital information in a notebook and hid it in my bedroom. These drugs were still at the experimental stage. The consequences for the individual's health, the contraindications with other drugs and the effect of long term damage, were unknown. Even the elite neuro-scientists could not be certain that I would retain mundane memories. It was quite possible that I could lose my sense of self. It was very concerning. But I knew I'd be investigated by the police... possibly with severe interrogation. In their eyes, I was still Mafia and what they wanted was to pin this murder on the Mafia so they could claim a huge victory. I had to ingest the drugs.

I was aware that time was my enemy and so were the Geneva police. I ate a high carbohydrate dinner as instructed and drank two full glasses of water. I undressed and prepared for bed at eight o'clock. Then, just before I put out the light, I swallowed the drugs.

My sleep was interspersed with lucid dreams. But eventually I awoke, still knowing who and where I was. The relief was overwhelming.

*

"Gilda, you were so brave," I said.

"No, Frances, not brave, my dear. It was a necessary task, to prevent my going to prison for the rest of my life, or perhaps facing the death penalty, depending on where I would be tried. There was a chance that I would face life without a cognitive functioning brain… I didn't want to know the odds. It was like a game of Russian roulette." she explained giving me one of her resilient smiles.

*

I knew the police would call to interview me. The Swiss Secret Service had already marked me as the wife of the Sorrentino godfather. I immediately read and learned the relatable account of my trip to LA so I'd be word perfect. Only the innocuous part of the trip remained in my mind, encoded as my new and true memory. I also sent Mario and Sergio out of town for a couple of weeks. It made things less complicated.

The Swiss Secret Service , SS/S, arrived early, around 6 a.m. the following day. In 1997, the SS/S was actually the National Security Council, which encompasses the relevant Secret Service and intelligence organizations run by the Swiss government. It wasn't until 2010 that the Swiss merged their agencies and formed a new security policy instrument in Switzerland, the Federal Intelligence Service, FIS.

I was still wearing my night clothes, but of course I let them enter.

"Gilda Sorrentino," one agent asked. "We'd like to ask you some questions about Michael Allen."

"I read about his suicide in the news and my name's not Sorrentino. I've reverted to my maiden name, Karter," I replied and showed them into the living room.

"How long were you married to Michael Allen?" asked one of the detectives.

"I was never married to him," I said. "I used to *tell* people I was married to Michael, in those days, as it was more acceptable than saying we were living together."

"You filed complaints of assault against him?"

"Yes, he physically abused and assaulted me," I said.

"So you killed him." One of the agents was trying to be clever.

"The abuse was thirty years ago. If I'd wanted to kill him, I'd have acted sooner," I said.

He ignored my answer. "When did you last see him?" he asked.

"Actually, it was at Geneva airport a couple of weeks ago. I had just arrived home from Amsterdam and he was walking to his gate on the other side of the dividing glass panel." I said.

"Why did you recently visit LA?" the other agent asked.

"I had a business commitment," I answered.

"Quite a coincidence, don't you agree, to be in LA at the time of Allen's murder?"

"As I said, it was business," I reiterated.

"Mafia business, was it?"

"As you can see, I'm separated from my husband, Beni Sorrentino. I have my own life now and my own business." I handed him my card.

"Where were you, on the night of Michael Allen's death?" asked the Swiss SS.

"I was attending a business function at a private house. I can verify that." I turned and handed him the invitation with the printed address. "My client can vouch for my attendance," I stated.

The detective glanced at the gilt-edged invitation and murmured his displeasure.

"Michael Allen's death was not suicide. It had the stamp of a Mafia execution all over it," he said.

I feigned disinterest, .

"You know what it's like when a dog pees at every tree in the park, well this is similar. The Mafia leave their trade mark… but you know all about that, don't you?" he said.

I ignored his rancid remark. "What do you want from me?" I asked.

"We'd like you to come along to our headquarters and make a statement," the agent said.

"Why don't you first check out my alibi? There are numerous people and staff who can attest to my presence at the party, including the CIA, who were following me during my visit. Once you've checked all the boxes, I'll contact my lawyer and make a statement," I said, firmly.

With that, they left my house. But I knew they'd return.

The following day they again arrived early at 6.am.

"Have you come to arrest me?" I enquired.

"The LAPD have forwarded their assessment of the crime and they're convinced it's the work of the Mafia," the detective stated.

"So why is that relevant to me?"

"Oh come on Gilda, you're Mafia!"

"No, I'm not!" I said. "Now let me ask you a question. If you think Michael Allen's death is a Mafia murder, why don't you suspect the Mickey Mouse Mafia in LA?"

"We're assured that it's not them... not their mark."

"Ah, yes, of course, I should have realized!" I said. "You have connections to the LA Mafia... top officials on the pad, are they?"

The agents ignored my remark. "There's one more thing," said one of the agents. "You were seen on camera, visiting the hospital room of Heidi Farve, the young woman that Michael Allen recently assaulted."

"I was concerned about her, after I read about her assault in the news. Is *that* now a crime too?" I said, testing him.

"This is all a little too perfect," said the other agent.

"Gilda Sorrentino..."

"Karter!" I corrected him.

"We require that you accompany us to our official headquarters to make a statement." said the senior agent.

"I'll telephone my lawyer," I answered.

*

"Gilda, I don't understand. You had an alibi from the CIA. Surely they'd confirm your attendance at the party, so why did you even need to take the drugs?" I asked.

"The CIA were never going to offer an alibi to a Mafia queen," Gilda replied.

"But they're a reputable agency... they're CIA," I said.

"Huh! They're corrupt. They're thick with the Mickey Mouse Mafia in LA and they'd pin the murder on me just for the glory of the headline news. I can visualize it now... Mafia queen arrested for murder. You have to understand, Frances, that the police and the agencies are embedded in corruption," she said. "They are never held accountable for their criminally duplicitous behavior."

"I'm sorry," I said, "I must seem so naive. Even though I spent time living with the Mafia, I never thought..."

"No need to be sorry, Frances. You spent only a fraction of your life with the Mafia, whereas I was ensconced in the *Family*. I'm well trained." Gilda laughed, and offered a moment of relief from this depressing truth.

*

I called my lawyer, who met me at the secret service headquarters. We talked privately and he was convinced of my innocence. Remember, he knew nothing about the drugs, so everything I relayed was *true*. I made a statement with details of my visit to LA, my business associates, the party and my return trip home. But still, the agents didn't believe me. They insisted I take a polygraph test.

I didn't resist. All I had to do was tell the truth... my later version, of course.

The procedure after that was very simple. My lawyer and I sat in a room with a dual screen... one of those two-way windows where expert psychologists watch you from the adjacent room. They wired me up and began to question me.

"What is your name?" they asked. "How old are you? What was the purpose of your recent trip to LA?" They ask questions that they know I'll answer truthfully and then they slip in a question which they hope will throw up a change and produce a different pattern on the polygraph. They watch for a rise in blood pressure, an increased pulse reading and any other physical reaction which can be measured. On and on they went, repeating question after question.

It soon became obvious that they weren't getting the result they expected. My pulse didn't race, my heart didn't pound and all my answers were truthful... because in my mind, they were.

They left me alone with my lawyer, in that room, for ten minutes. Probably, they were conferring with the psychologists, watching us through the screen and listening in the hope of hearing something that would incriminate me. But of course, there was nothing. I had no memory of Michael Allen except the detailed account that I'd learnt *after* I ingested the drugs. I was innocent.

My lawyer demanded they end this charade without further delay. The agents had failed to find any incriminating evidence for which to arrest me for the murder of Michael Allen. They knew my alibi would stand up if ever this were to go to trial, and they had no grounds for arrest. My lawyer and I left unhindered and I went back to my life.

The next day, I visited Heidi and her father. They'd heard the news of Michael Allen's fall to his death. Heidi expressed relief that he would never again be a threat to her or any other woman. Her father just smiled and gave me a nod.

"Thank you, Gilda. You're a woman of your word." He shook my hand and as promised, he asked no questions.

*

"So Gilda, tell me, are we writing this part of your life based on the notes you made before you lost this memory?" I asked.

"Yes, Frances. When I read these words from my journal, it's as if they happened to someone else. I still have no personal memory of the traumatic events surrounding Michael Allen," she said. "But envisaging the assault happening to any woman would make me feel desperately sad. Ingesting the fact that I had experienced the reality of this event is in itself truly traumatic."

"I assume you've had no reaction to the drugs?" I added.

"It's late, my dear." Gilda purposely glanced at her Swiss grandfather clock. "Forgive me, but I'm rather tired. I think I'll retire early tonight."

I agreed and wished her goodnight. Noting that she'd consciously avoided answering my question.

Mixed Emotions
Day Sixteen

"Good morning Gilda. Are you feeling refreshed today?" I asked her.

"Good morning Frances, yes I'm fit for another day's storytelling," she said.

*

The year was 1998 and I was fifty-one years old. I decided to move to a larger house. I'm a great believer in timing... as you know, so when I began my search I was certain in my heart that the perfect home was waiting for me, right here in Carouge.

I'd often passed the house with the pale pink washed walls and thought how well it would suit me. We both know that there are no accidents in life, so I was not surprised when the real estate agent contacted me about a house that was about to enter the market. I'd become a fixture in this small town and I wanted to remain in the center with all its familiarity.

The house was adjacent to the market square, set amongst the shops and cafés, but it had a private garden at the rear, which I wanted. It would not have been safe for me to live in an isolated rural area. I was still vulnerable and my head could command a tidy ransom for other clans with a grievance against the Sorrentinos.

I closed the deal quickly and moved into this beautiful building. Most importantly, it had two side apartments; one for the soldato who would be my bodyguard, and the other for a childless couple from Sorrento, whom I'd known for twenty years. We'd bonded soon after I'd arrived in Italy. They were victims of a tragic incident. Their young son was caught in crossfire during a raid and killed instantly. At the time all I could do was to offer them comfort and support. Later, when I proposed that they join me in Carouge, they literally jumped at the chance. I was grateful for their loyalty and for them, a change of scenery was overdue. Estela was to be my housekeeper and her older husband, Alberto, would see to the upkeep of the house and the garden. They, like me, could leave those nightmare memories of murder behind and start anew.

I had many friends in Carouge and I liked to entertain, so engaging a housekeeper was a huge bonus. We both liked to cook and had much fun in the kitchen. The simplicity of those moments was necessary after so much trauma in our lives.

I spent the following nine years enjoying my life, my friends and my work. Then in 2007 tragedy hit again. Beni had suffered a stroke. His whole right side was paralyzed. He couldn't move his right arm, leg or even the right side of his face… poor Beni.

I immediately travelled to Sorrento. It nearly broke my heart to see this proud man incapacitated. Dino organized twenty-four hour nursing and with physical therapy, Beni gained some movement, but he was basically immobilized. He was very depressed, so I sat with him for days, trying to add some purpose to his life. I read to him, relayed the news and chatted about the *Family*. He tried hard to communicate: his speech was slurred, but he managed to talk. We reminisced about the time we met and our first years together. He told me he'd never stopped loving me and I told him the same. For me, that was not entirely true. But, there was a part of me that still loved him, as a friend.

It was strange to be back in Sorrento. I loved the town, but not the Mafia stronghold. Dino tried to persuade me to return and care for Beni. He said I should fulfil my duty as Beni's wife — until death us do part. But I reminded him that Beni had replaced me with his Mafia "wife" and she and his children would surround him with the love and care he needed.

When I said goodbye to Beni, he grabbed my arm with his able hand and stared hard into my eyes. It seemed as though he was saying… if only? That is something we all think, but should never say. I smiled, kissed him and told him he'd been a good husband and a good man. The left side of his mouth began to curl, forming a half smile as he exerted a huge effort to respond to my reassurance. We held each other in a prolonged mutual gaze and shared our last precious moments. I left that day.

My trip to Italy had been unsettling and I was pleased to return home to Carouge. I had moved on with my life. The Mafia and Sorrento belonged to a previous life, from which I was now estranged.

*

During the next few years, I worked relentlessly, travelling around Europe, networking with the gold and diamond traders. My diamonds were mainly bought in Amsterdam, but I enjoyed a few trips to South

Africa meeting dealers in Johannesburg. There was, at this time, a surge of blood diamonds, so called because they were mined in war zones and sold to finance insurgencies. I was always particular about their source and avoided buying from the African nations involved. I had a reputation to preserve, and there were numerous fake certificates accompanying these gems. So, I only bought from reputable dealers. Diamonds were secondary to me. My preference was for gold… it was my prime commodity and the love of my life… in non-human form.

I was at peace with myself. My life was blissful and so I postponed the nagging issue that I vowed to address. I felt that I'd be tempting fate to destroy my life again. I ignored my conscience until an event prompted me to realize that it was time to act.

The year was 2013 and I was sixty-six years old, when I received a call from Dino. Beni had suffered a fatal stroke and I was summoned back to Sorrento for the funeral.

I was collected at Naples airport, just like the old days, and driven to Sorrento. I never tired of the magnificent views along the twisting road that led up to the mansions. The bright Italian light reflected on the white washed walls and the aroma of spring flowers bursting with the anticipation of life. But it was death that had called me back, and I felt its depression as I entered the compound.

I made my way to the main hall and felt the memories of my first visit to this old house come flooding back. Beni's coffin was situated in the center, with the sunlight falling on half of the casket. It mirrored the state of his body during his last years — half of it motionless and unyielding and the other still mobile and vigorous. A penalty which lasted too long for a proud man such as Beni to endure.

Dino approached me and greeted me in the Italian way, with a kiss on each cheek. "Gilda, good of you to come," he said. "You look older."

"So do you," I replied. "He hung on a long time," I remarked and gestured towards the casket.

"He is with our dear parents now," Dino replied.

"And Nonno and Nonna too," I reminded him.

"I remember how close you were to Nonno when you lived in this house, Gilda, " said Dino. "We were both so young. "

"And now we are the old ones," I told him.

The funeral was to be held at the chapel inside the compound. The security was tight but manageable and the outsiders who attended were carefully vetted. Funerals were notorious for raids by opposing clans. Some of the older godfathers came and paid their respects. I remembered them and they me. We nodded in unison.

As I entered the chapel I walked forward to greet the rest of the family. I was taken aback by the similarity of Beni's son to his father... it quite startled me. He looked as Beni had looked when he was young; broad, tall and handsome. They were all assembled, including his Mafia "wife". How she must have despised my presence as the lawful wife, when she'd been with him all these years and given birth to his children. I hoped she didn't resent me, so I purposely took a pew behind her as a mark of my respect.

It was a sad day, but made lighter by Beni's last wish. It was for the family to dine at Ristorante Museo Caruso. My first visit to Caruso's famous restaurant had also been bitter-sweet. It was after the assassination of Beni's uncle, when the whole family assembled for the initiation of the joint godfathers; Beni and Dino. They are, to this day, the only twins to inherit this position in Mafia history. The Sorrentino Padrini.

Tradition is big in Italy, like gestures and generosity. After we'd eaten delicious Italian food and drunk more than our share of red wine, the volume on the old fashioned gramophone, which played Caruso's music, was turned up as a hint that it was time to leave and head home to bed.

My Italian life had ended as it began and now, I finally had closure. As the car sped along the winding road heading for the airport, I looked back one last time at my beautiful Sorrento. My thoughts mingled with memories of love and sadness, death and sorrow.

I was officially a widow and it was a freedom I embraced. Now I could address the issue which had been nagging at my conscience for many years. I could search for my son.

*

I'd been hesitant to search for Gary while Beni was alive. There'd always been the chance that he'd discover my secret and realize that it was my fault we'd had a childless marriage. As it was, Beni had assumed that God had intervened and deemed us incompatibly infertile. The miracle that I'd prayed for didn't happen. The doctors were correct in their diagnosis, that I would never have children after that fateful assault.

I began by contacting an agency that specialized in reuniting birth mothers with their adopted children. The last I knew of Gary was that he went to loving Catholic parents. I didn't know the family's last name, the only information I had was Gary's date of birth.

It took a long time before we had any leads. Then one day I received a phone call.

"Mrs. Karter?" the woman's voice enquired. She had an American accent and I remember the feeling of goose bumps as I answered.

"Yes," I replied.

"I think we have a match for your son Gary," she said. "We firstly identified him by the last name, it's the same as yours. For some reason, he chose to revert to the name on his birth certificate, Carter. We're aware that the spelling of a last name is often changed during an adoption process, just as it was with immigrants entering through Ellis Island. So we matched Carter with Karter and I'm pleased to tell you that we're sure Gary Carter is your son."

I was completely overcome with emotion, I couldn't speak, just sobbed. Finally, I asked how I should proceed and was told that I'd receive details in the mail. But I was also warned that Gary may not want to contact me.

"Sometimes the children resent the parents, for obvious reasons. Are you prepared for a disappointment?" She asked.

I murmured that I understood. But my excitement overruled any rational thought.

Now I was instructed to wait. Gary would be approached by the agency and given my telephone number. I was ecstatic.

*

"Gilda, you'd lived separately from Beni for many years. Was that the real reason you delayed your search for Gary?" I boldly asked.

"You're very perceptive, Frances. My main reason for delaying was fear. I was too afraid," she replied.

"Afraid of what?"

"Afraid that my son would judge me and so I left it until—"" she paused in reflection. "Until I became aware of my mortality," she said.

All my previous suspicions about Gilda's state of health seem to loom before me after hearing this statement. So I suggested a break for lunch.

*

I eventually received the long awaited phone call, but it was not from Gary. The woman from the agency called with some disturbing news.

"The good news is that your son Gary is willing to make contact. The bad news is… and I'm sorry to tell you… he's in prison," she said.

I was filled with mixed emotion. "What's he done?" I asked.

"He's serving a thirteen year sentence for…" she hesitated before explaining. "For murder," she blurted out. "I'm so sorry," she added.

I was stunned! After all these years of thinking about him and how he'd developed… to find out that he was in prison! It was unreal. However, I noted the address and the fact that he wanted to meet me, and sat down to make my decision.

*

"Well Frances, the rest you know, but I'll go over it again. It was of course shortly before we met," Gilda said.

"Yes, I remember it clearly," I replied.

*

I flew to LA and made an appointment to visit Gary. I was shaking… I didn't know what to expect. It was possible that he would hate me on sight. Maybe he'd hurl insults at me for giving him up for adoption. All kinds of questions were flooding my mind.

"Gary?" I said, as I sat down in front of the screen.

"So you're my mother?" these were his opening words.

I nodded. "How are you doing?" I asked.

He looked at me and with a smile, he answered. "Pretty good, this place is like a vacation camp" and he laughed. "Just so you know… I'm innocent. I didn't fucking kill her." He was angry. "They locked me away but I swear that when I fucking get out of here I'm gonna find that detective and burn him!"

"The detective? " I questioned.

"Yeah, the motherfucker who put me in this hell hole," he replied.

"I'm so sorry, Gary. But let's talk about us," I said, changing the subject. "I'm just pleased to see you after all these years. Tell me, did your adopted family treat you well? Did they love you?"

"They were okay, but too obsessed with God. I was a pretty normal kid, got into all kind'a stuff. But everything I did was labeled *evil*. I had two adopted siblings and we were all punished as *sinners* according to our parents. You know, they beat us. I couldn't take it, so when I turned sixteen, I left home."

My eyes began to sting with tears. But I swallowed my grief and explained why I'd given him up and what happened to me at the hands of his father. "Do you blame me for what I did?" I asked. I *had* to ask, but was dreading his answer.

Gary sat and thought before he spoke. He was obviously intelligent and his answer surprised me.

"I wouldn't have had a child at twenty-one, I'd have had the girl get an abortion," he said.

"I couldn't have done that... I wanted to keep you, but your father—"

"Yeah, don't fret. You did okay," he said.

It was the best answer I could hope for, in the circumstances.

I stayed in LA for some time and visited Gary regularly so I could get to know him and offer moral support. He told me about his marriage to Lauren and his arrest after she died. When I heard that her journal was to be auctioned, I knew I had to acquire it. I wanted to read how Lauren had described her husband... my son. I suppose I wanted to find out the truth. Was my son a murderer? I wasn't sure.

I attended the auction solely to acquire Lauren Carter's journal, because I wanted to read about my son. Even if it was loathsome, he was still my son... carrying my genes.

*

"And that's when I first laid eyes on you Frances, at the auction," said Gilda.

"I remember it well," I said, "and how we competed fiercely for Lauren's journal."

"Yes my dear, and you won," she said.

"When we met in LA it was obvious you had money, and so I remember asking why you didn't outbid me," Frances said. "You answer was intriguing."

"Yes, I told you that it was sheer conceit. I glimpsed something of myself in you. I turned around in that auction room and saw myself as a younger woman, standing in your place. You bid with such intensity that I thought you'd have killed me, rather than lose the journal," Gilda said. "And here we are... such is life."

*

When you published your book, based on Lauren's notes and also titled *The Journal*, I rushed out and bought it. I gave a copy to my son. But he objected to your portrayal of her murder with recurring flares of anger. I really didn't know how to handle it.

I remained a frequent visitor while he was in prison. He seemed to enjoy our reconnection, but once he was released, I hardly saw him… and then he died. I didn't like him. He was a despicable, reprehensible person but as a mother, I loved him.

*

"Gilda, when Gary pursued me, I was terrified. Do you remember that the threats began when he found out that I was living with the detective who was responsible for his arrest?" I said.

"I remember you telling me the whole story when you arrived at my home in Geneva. The linking of our lives is uncanny. Perhaps even karmic," she said. "I still don't understand why Dino's Mafiosi murdered Gary. It was a rookie soldato… so I'm told. But why was he mixed up with the Mafia? No one in the *Family* knew he was my son." Gilda looked despondent.

Was this the moment to reveal my secrets? I'd chosen to withhold information about Gary's death from Gilda when we were in LA. I never thought that I'd have to divulge that now… but perhaps it would help? Looking at her sad expression…would it bring closure? Or would it break the bond of trust we'd forged? I shook myself out of my dilemma and decided my confession could wait.

"I'm not sure I believe in karma," I said.

"You surprise me, Frances. When we've finished this biography I'll highlight all the areas of my life in which karma has played its part," Gilda said, with a smile that portrayed the wisdom of her years.

"I think we're almost done," I told her. "According to our notes, we have only a few lose ends to tie up."

"Then I'll retire early today. I've a slight headache and need to lie down. I'll see you in the morning, my dear. Goodnight," she said.

The Visitor
Day Seventeen

"Good morning, Gilda," I said. But for her, it obviously wasn't. She was sitting in the corner chair by the window and the daylight made her look quite pale. "Are you alright?" I asked.

"I have a persistent headache," she said, "I've struggled with it all night."

"Would you like me to fetch some aspirin ?" I offered.

She lowered her head and placed her hand on her forehead. "I've taken something a little stronger... oh, I'm feeling odd—" and she keeled over and collapsed onto the floor. "Estela! Help!" I yelled. Estela came running into the room.

"Oh my God!" she said, covering her mouth with her hand. "It's happened... she said it would, but I didn't want to believe her."

"What?" I said. "What's happened? What are you talking about?"

We gently laid her frail body on the couch and Estela called the doctor. I sat and held her hand in her unconscious state. "Tell me Estela," I pleaded.

"She told me not to tell you... but now, it's time for you to know," she said.

My mind was racing and recalling all those moments Gilda had felt tired and unwell.

"She has a brain tumor. It's inoperable. She knew the end was near and she made me promise not to breathe a word. She didn't want her health issues to affect the writing of the book. It's been so difficult, keeping her secret," Estela's voice broke and she began to cry.

It all made sense now. The rush to finish the book and her progressing frailty. Strange, I thought, how people seem to hang on until they're ready to say goodbye.

*

Gilda was transported directly to the hospital and whisked into the critical care unit. Estela and I sat outside and waited... and waited. Eventually a doctor spoke to us. "She's out of pain and as comfortable as can be expected. I suggest you both go home, get some rest and return tomorrow morning."

I couldn't sleep at all that night, so I read through the draft of the book. Many of Gilda's revelations were alarming and I'd been so concerned... I realized now why she was relaxed about the whistle-blowing. It reminded me of when I was a child in Amsterdam. My mother and I would spend our evenings engrossed in some complicated jigsaw. Then, quite suddenly, we'd place the last few pieces and the puzzle was complete.

The next day I was able to speak with the senior consultant in charge. He was a top neuro-surgeon and explained the situation, without disclosing the cause.

"Some months ago, we discovered a large tumor in Gilda's brain. It was growing rapidly and its position made it inoperable. She had a further brain scan last week which revealed two subsequent tumors. I'm sorry—" He paused, looked away and returned his gaze to face us. "I'm sorry to tell you, that she probably has only a few days to live."

Estela and I clung on to each other to withstand the agony of losing our beloved Gilda. I could no longer hold back the tears which stung my eyes and blurred my vision.

We sat until we were cried out, then we washed our faces and Estela departed. I forced a smile and prepared to visit Gilda.

*

I walked through the ward and opened the door of a private room. Gilda was half propped-up on pillows with an intravenous drip attached to her left arm. She smiled, and I donned a brave face as I entered.

"Hello my dear, sit here on the bed, I need to talk with you," she said. Her voice was weak and she looked frail. The strong character that had inhabited this small frame was diminishing before my eyes.

I complied with her wishes, sat down and took her hand in mine.

"I suppose by now you know the truth?" she enquired.

"Yes, the consultant explained... I'm so very sorry. Gilda. Why didn't you tell me? "

"You know why," she replied. "You'd have been concerned, we'd have slowed down the process and never finished the project... and the point is, it's done. The book's finished."

"Yes, it's finished. I proofread it last night and it's perfect... alarming, enlightening—"

"And *true*," she said. "The truth can't hurt me now. Promise me you'll publish it soon, Frances. I don't want anyone to beat me to it," she said with a wry smile.

"I'd never let that happen and besides, only you can tell your personal life story. As for the Mafia, no one else dare tell! You're a brave lady, Gilda," I said.

"Ah, not so. Dino can't hurt me when I'm dead," she said.

"Please don't say that."

"We both know it's true. Don't be sad, my dear, I did what I had to do," she said.

"Gilda, do they know what caused the tumors?" I asked.

"No, the doctors here don't know... but I do. When I took the drugs to erase the traumatic memory, I knew they were virtually untested and that there was a possibility of the formation of brain tumors as a result," she explained.

"Oh Gilda, was it worth it?"

"Yes, absolutely. I've arrived at an age where I can look back and say that I've really lived a full life. I've dealt with my grievances... in a big way!" she said and laughed. "Not many women have become a Mafia queen and few, I suspect, have had the blessing of a great love."

"I wish you could have seen David one last time," I said.

"I sensed that David died, a short while ago. One evening while I was lying in my bed I felt his presence. It was a feeling of complete love which surrounded me... it was almost tangible. I believe he'd come to say goodbye." Her eyes always glowed when she spoke of David. "He's travelled ahead of me and soon I'll know that road, too."

"I can't bear it," I said. "It's all so sad... what will I do?—"

"Listen carefully, my dear. You'll be sad for a while, it's only natural when someone we care about dies. But I want you to remember the joy. The times we laughed... make limoncello, have fun!"

I felt ashamed. Gilda was dying and here she was, comforting me.

"Frances, I have two serious requests which I entrust to you alone," she said.

"Of course, anything," I replied.

"The first is to mail a letter to the clinic I visited, regarding the memory-erasing drugs. I need them to know my prognosis, for their records. The second is to visit my lawyer. You'll find his address on the front of his letter and you'll find both envelopes in the drawer of my bedside table.

Thank you, my dear."

"Of course Gilda, I'd do anything for you. You've become a sister, a mother, a friend rolled into one," I said, again fighting back the tears.

"Frances, best you go now my dear," she said, gently squeezing my hand. "I need to rest. Be sure to drink a glass of that vintage port before you go to bed... it will help you sleep."

I kissed her goodbye and guessed that she knew I'd had a sleepless night. She knew me so well.

*

The following day, just as I was preparing to leave for the hospital, Estela knocked at my door.

"There's a young man at the main entrance, wanting to see Gilda," she said.

"Is he Mafia?" I enquired.

"Not sure. Mario's with him," she said.

"I'll come down," I replied, thinking how good it was to have Mario around and how I'd miss him.

Mario met me at the door. "He says he's from Alaska!" Mario said.

"Alaska? I don't know anyone from there."

I walked towards the young man standing in the porch. He was in his twenties, with dark hair, a gentle face and mesmerizing green eyes. He smiled as I approached.

"Gilda's not well," I said, offering my outstretched hand. "My name's Frances, can I help you?"

"I'm Luke," he said, gripping my hand firmly. "I'd hoped to meet Gilda... she was a close friend of my father."

It was then I became intrigued. "What's your father's name?" I asked.

"It's David... *was* David. Sadly, he died a couple of weeks ago," he said.

"I'm so sorry." My mind began to spin with the possibility that this was the son of Gilda's lover, David. "Would you like to come inside where we can talk?"

He followed me into the day room and I asked Estela to provide some coffee.

"Are you Gilda's daughter?" he asked.

"No, but I'm a close friend. I've been writing her biography and staying here during the process. I've heard about your father," I said. "But I have to ask if you have any proof that you're David's son?"

"Yes, I have my passport," which he handed to me.

"Your last name is not the same as the one Gilda mentioned?" I said.

"No, that's because my father changed his name... well, apparently, I read in his journal that he was given a new identity. Look... I have a code," he said, turning to the back page of the brown leather bound journal. "It says here that he and Gilda used this contact code between them... Open Sesame. My father said it came from her father."

"Yes, it did. He and Gilda devised it on her wedding day. Thank you, Luke. The code is correct. I'm so pleased you're here," I said. "Please tell me more."

"My father had been ill for some time, but just before he died, he entrusted me with his journal. He told me he'd had an interesting life before I was born and said I should read it after he died. I was born in Alaska, we had a quiet existence, hunting, fishing, running a small business. I had no idea that he'd lived a completely different life before he married my mother." He looked quite bewildered. "I found this address written inside the journal and I just had to come. Gilda was the love of his life... is it possible to meet her?"

"I know she'd love to meet you. Grab your coat and I'll explain on the way to the hospital," I told him.

"Hospital?" Luke repeated.

"Yes, miraculously, you're just in time!" I said, smiling at the irony of life.

In the car, Luke described his amazement at the covert life his father and Gilda had led while working together. How they'd risked their lives against the Mafia clans in New Jersey in order to help others.

"Yes, they were a brave couple. They succeeded in cleansing a large area from persecution and racketeering," I said.

"They loved each other deeply, didn't they?"

"It was a very special love. A once in a lifetime affair," I replied.

*

I peered into Gilda's room. She was awake and smiled when she saw me. "How are you today?" I asked.

"All the better for seeing you my dear," she said. Her voice was soft and her energy was low.

"I've brought someone special to see you... he's no ordinary visitor," I told her.

"Ummm, I'm curious. I know that you wouldn't bring just *anyone*.

They must be important," she said.

"He is," I said and opened the door.

Luke walked through the door and before he reached the bed, Gilda spoke.

"I know those eyes. They belong to your father," she said and a solitary tear rolled down her cheek as she reached out for Luke's hand.

"Yes Gilda, I have my father's eyes... you're very perceptive. It's so wonderful to meet you," Luke said, taking her hand and gently kissing it.

"He's dead, isn't he?"

"He died a couple of weeks ago and that's when I acquired *this*." He placed his father's brown leather-bound journal in her hand.

Gilda caressed the cover as if it were David's own hand. She opened it tenderly and ran her fingers along the sentences written with his pen.

"I've learnt all about you both. About the life my father led before I was born and about the love he had for you, Gilda. He placed you on a pedestal and I can see why." Luke's words touched Gilda's heart.

"You look so much like your father when he was young. Tell me Luke, was he happy?"

"He was, but there was always a reserve about him. Some part of his personality that he withheld. I never really knew what it was... but now I do. It was a pining for you Gilda and the sadness of lost love."

I watched them both bond in a shared memory of a loved one. The wonder of this moment, remembering their individual feelings for a man so loved, was one I would treasure for the rest of my life. It's true, that love never dies. Its immortality exists in the hearts and minds of the people we love and who love us in return.

"My father used to sit in the dark and listen to Verdi's opera, *Rigoletto*... he loved it as the name Gilda belongs to one of the characters," Luke told her.

"You've made me very happy," Gilda said. "Now my dears, it's time for you both to leave me with these sweet memories."

"I'm pleased they can console you Gilda," I said.

"Not console my dear. This is my time to *rejoice*. I love you both."

We each kissed her goodbye and as I left, I noticed that she had exchanged her depleted energy for a radiant glow.

*

Our leaving the hospital was bitter-sweet. Seeing Gilda happy in such dire circumstances was due to Luke's appearance and so it seemed appropriate to invite him to stay the night in Gilda's home, instead of a hotel.

We sat in the sitting room talking until the sunlight disappeared behind the church, which cast a shadow across our windows. The emotions of the day had drained us and so we filled our stomachs with a hearty dinner, accompanied by a bottle of red wine. Luke was young... barely mid-twenties. But his mind appeared older than his years. He'd attended the university in Anchorage and obtained an engineering degree, and his accumulated general knowledge made him an interesting guest. He spoke lovingly of his father, his home and his state.

"Will you stay in Alaska?" I asked.

"Yeah, if I can. I can't imagine living in the lower forty-eight." He laughed. "I expect you've heard that term before. Up there, we're a breed apart from the rest of the US."

"The lower forty-eight, yes, I've heard that before. But Alaska is too cold for me," and I proceeded to talk about my life in California and Italy, and how I'd met Gilda.

"I've talked too much," I told him. "Tell me about your life with your father."

"Dad and I spent much of our time outdoors. Alaska's a wondrous natural state, where we could be as one with nature. He taught me how to hunt and fish, but he also taught me about the preservation of life. We never killed an animal unless it was for food. We would always use all of it. With moose, we'd also use the hide. We'd fish for salmon and make stock from the bones. I'm a child of the land, I couldn't imagine being cooped up inside a house, writing at a desk like you Frances."

"Did you read books?" I enquired.

"Yes, my father had a mixture of the classics and contemporary novels. The evenings were long and so we read and played games," Luke said.

"You don't talk about your mother."

"She left when I was twelve. Ran off with some man and moved to California. I never saw her again."

"I'm sorry."

"I'm not. I enjoyed life with my father. But now there's a huge hole in my heart and I miss him." He spoke sadly and sniffed.

I leaned forward and touched his hand in an attempt to comfort him.

He placed his on top of mine in a return gesture and we registered a moment of tenderness. We were two lost souls, seeking solace in the other.

"Do you have friends? A girlfriend perhaps?" I enquired.

"There was a girl, but nothing serious. And yes, I have a load of friends," he said.

After dinner we moved into the sitting room and Luke made for the chess table.

"In his journal, my dad wrote that he and Gilda played chess. Do you play, Frances?"

"Yes, want a game?" I suggested, thinking it would be a distraction from our grief.

"Sure," he agreed. "I'll set up the board."

We sat opposite each other and I chose white, so mine was the first move.

"e4," I moved my pawn into the center of the board.

"e5, there Frances, we are face to face," said Luke moving his black pawn.

"Nf3." I moved my knight forward into an attack position.

"Ah Frances, you're attacking my pawn," Luke said. "f6."

"Ummm. I see you're playing defensively," I said, thinking that f7 was wide open. "Nxe5"

"So, you want my king? fxe5." Luke's move was consistent with his last, but unwise. He looked intensely at me.

"Qh5+... check."

"You're dangerous. Ke7." Luke continued to stare at me.

"Are you trying to unnerve me?" I said, "Qxe5+."

"Yes," he said, "Kf7," moving his hand across the table and letting his fingertips touch mine.

"Bc4+." My move was one-handed. The other remained attached to Luke's by the pads of my fingers.

"d5." Luke repositioned his hand on top of mine, pinning it to the table. "Your move," he said.

"Check... Bxd5+. Now *you* can't move," I said.

"Yes I can, Frances, but I'm unsure how you'll react," Luke said.

"Try me," I replied, fixing him with my eyes.

He pushed back his chair and now holding my hand, walked around the table and gently pulled me out of my seat. We stood face to face, just as when we'd begun our chess game. But this game was different.

"K+Q… I have you in check, Frances," he said.

"QxK# … checkmate," I replied — and then he kissed me.

His lips were tender, as first kisses often are. He paused, looked closely into my eyes for reassurance. I smiled, walked toward the door and locked it.

"Frances, I think you're an amazing woman," Luke whispered in my ear as he wrapped his arms around me.

"I'm much older than you—"

Luke placed his finger against my lips to silence my words. "Age is irrelevant… people matter, *we* matter," he said. "At times like this, we must live in the moment."

I looked into his young face, but I didn't see his youth. I saw only his loving eyes glowing with desire, and mine mirrored his. He pulled me down onto the thick white rug that lay in front of the open fire. With gentle movements, he peeled off my clothes layer by layer, all the time fixing me with his magnetic green eyes until we lay together naked; our skin warmed by the heat from the flames and our hearts fired by our passion. It was obvious that this was not a physical act alone. Our souls connected as deeply as our bodies. I gave no thought to the twenty years difference in our ages. Seduction surpasses age. I was as much a seductress as he a seducer and we held each other captive, locked into our intimate embrace. Over and over we rolled, our sweating flesh slipping and sliding against the other, navigating our sexuality across every erogenous zone until finally we lay apart, exhausted and motionless.

I turned my head and looked into his hypnotic green eyes. They were more than a mere aphrodisiac… they reflected a deep and significant human being, with good values.

"You look radiant Frances," Luke said as he tenderly kissed me.

I just smiled at this beautiful young man. We had expended our emotions, our sexuality and further conversation was unnecessary. We had shared a moment of bliss and not wanting to diminish this memory, I chose to end it. I gathered my clothes, gently kissed Luke goodnight and went to my bed, alone.

*

At 8 am. there was a call from the hospital. Gilda had died peacefully in her sleep and without pain. I dissolved into tears.

After I'd dressed, I went downstairs to announce the news to Estela and Luke. Estela cried and Luke was much saddened, but grateful for his brief encounter with his father's lover. We had breakfast, mainly coffee, as we were too sad to eat.

"I have much to arrange," I said. "Gilda had left instructions regarding her funeral. It's going to be heart-wrenching, but I'll do my best," I said.

"If you need me to help, I could delay—"

"No, that's not necessary. I know you need to get home and see to your father's arrangement too," I told him.

"Strange, isn't it? That after all these years, they should both die within a matter of days," Luke observed.

"Do you believe they're together at last?" I asked.

"I don't know what I believe, but I'd like to think that they are," Luke replied.

We joined hands across the table. "I'll think of you often," I said.

"And I you," said Luke.

*

The funeral was conducted at the Catholic church, at Gilda's request. I wondered whether I should contact the rabbi, as Gilda was technically Jewish, but decided that would complicate matters. The last memory of Gilda in Carouge should not be a competition of faiths.

Estela and I walked together behind the coffin, clutching each other's arm for comfort and steadiness. It was almost two years since Estela's husband, Alberto, had been carried along this route too.

The village turned out in numbers greater than I'd anticipated. She was much admired and loved. I delivered the eulogy, without eluding to her previous life as a Mafia queen. But I did mention the soon-to-be-published biography and then, all who dared to read would know.

After the service, we gathered at a local restaurant, where about fifty friends joined us for refreshments and a much needed jolt of alcohol.

I surveyed the unfamiliar faces of her placid friends. All looked sad and controlled. I thought how different this experience seemed from the Italian funerals Gilda had described.

I leaned towards Estela to make a statement, "I think Gilda would have preferred Caruso's!"

The Last Revelation
Day Twenty-Eight

It wasn't until after the funeral that I picked up the white envelope, which Gilda had left for me, and ran my fingers over my hand-written name. Her fragile writing wavered and tapered off at the end of Frances. Inside, was a letter which had obviously been written before she became too ill to steady a pen.

'My dear Frances,

I am about to reveal the last revelation and the one I feel to be the greatest of all. It will come as a shock, so do sit down my dear.

The story begins with my father and his brother. As you know through your transcribing of my life, my father and mother fled to Amsterdam before the Second World War. His brother, my uncle, had emigrated to America and settled in Minnesota. They exchanged letters before the war, but during those desperate war-torn years, they had no contact. It was only after the war that the letters began to flow again. The news of my uncle was that he had married and had a son, who was a few years older than me. Unfortunately, the last letter to reach my parents was that from the son Hank, when he was only eighteen, informing them of his father's death. That young man, my parents' nephew and my first cousin, enlisted in the navy.

When we emigrated to America in 1964, we decided to settle in Minnesota and search for the family. My father contacted the navy and was given an address in Colorado. They received a reply from his young wife, who informed them Hank was serving overseas and would contact them when he was next on leave. Unfortunately, my parents were killed soon after and I lost touch with my cousin.

The story could have ended there, but something drove me to trace the family after I'd contacted Gary. Possibly it was a longing for family connections or blood ties. I noticed that recently I'd felt the urge to find out what happened to them… I couldn't explain it. But I searched and this is what I found.

My cousin Hank married a woman who was an ex-nun. They had two daughters, Mary and Frances. By now my dear, you're probably filling in the rest of the story.'

A chill ran down my spine as I again read the names... Mary and Frances.

My mother had entered a convent at the tender age of eighteen. I had photos of her as a novice, dressed all in white. She became a Bride of Christ after the requisite four years and then she had a crisis. She struggled on for a few years and finally left the Order. Her will to serve humankind was redirected to the navy, where she trained as a nurse, met my father... and we were born.

I never knew my paternal grandfather, but I remembered my parents talking about his journey to America and how he'd escaped the Nazi rising in Austria. He traveled through Italy and took passage on a cargo vessel at the port of Naples, bound for New York.

I read on.

'As you now know, your father and I were first cousins, although we never met. We, my dear Frances, are second cousins. But the greatest revelation is that my grandparents were your great-grandparents. To some, this is an unbelievable story... but for us, life is different. Do you remember what I told you, shortly after you arrived at my home, here in Geneva?'

I shuddered as I read her words.

'It will be interesting to see if our genetic footprints have trodden the same road, somewhere in our past. If it's true that our ancestry reveals a shared DNA, we would have inherited the same past family experiences that influence our decisions and actions today. Through our forefathers, the consequences of our present lives were already set in our genes several generations ago.'

My head was spinning. I paused and took some deep breaths before I continued to read the next page.

'As my only living relative...' my heart skipped a beat as I read this in black and white... *'you, my dear Frances, will inherit my estate. Everything is in order so the transition will be smooth and fast. I have left Estela a pension and hopefully she'll stay with you a while, before she retires.*

The keys and passwords to my deposit boxes are locked in a small safe hidden in the wall, behind the oil painting in my bedroom. I hope you like gold?'

I remembered when I had first set eyes on Gilda in LA. It was at the auction where I obtained Lauren's journal. I'd named her Goldie, due to her excessive gold jewelry. My instinct had been correct, but I hadn't known to what extent gold had impacted her life. She had chosen the Earth's treasures… diamonds and gold, as her merchandise. She was indeed a *woman of gold*, with a relevant name.

Gilda continued: '*Once our book of revelations is published, the disclosure clause I wrote should exonerate you from the revelations within… they are entirely my thoughts which I have chosen to make public. If Dino protests, remember my dear, stand strong and remind him that you are only the messenger. Although that is not strictly true.*'

This was a lot to take in and my mind was racing with questions.

'*It must be clear to you by now why we couldn't include this information in our book. The only person who knows that you are a blood relative is my lawyer. No one else must know this truth, especially Dino. As a relative of a Mafia queen who betrayed the Family, you are vulnerable. Remember our Family law, our code of conduct… an eye for an eye—. Retribution will be inflicted on or by a relative. You are my only living relative… be forever vigilant my dear.*'

Karma
Day One Hundred & Forty

It had been one hundred and forty days since I began transcribing Gilda's memoirs. I still kept count. And it was one hundred and twenty days since her death. Over four months had passed and I was still grieving. I was in limbo and I'd taken to drinking a copious amount of red wine at dinner, to blot out the sadness and entice sleep.

This particular morning I awoke early, jolted out of a deep and necessary sleep. I lay still for a few minutes and listened. I heard doors open and close and assumed it was Estela preparing breakfast. I glanced at the clock; it was only 5 am. so I slid under the duvet to catch another hour's rest.

Crash! The noise was alarming, but probably the trill sound was only that of cutlery landing on the tiled kitchen floor. Crash! There it was again and this time I couldn't return to rest. I grabbed a bath robe and made my way down the stairs.

"Estela!" I called, as I drew nearer the kitchen, but there was no answer. I swung open the kitchen door, half expecting to see her collapsed on the floor, but only the cutlery lay strewn before my feet, scattered across the terracotta tiles. "Estela!" I called again. The aroma of coffee hung in the air, but the coffee pot was missing. I felt the metal percolator... it was still warm.

Something was wrong. Mario had left and Estela and I were the sole occupants of the house... and the early morning coffee was not for me. Or perhaps it was? She may have been en route to my room, when suddenly taken ill and run to the bathroom.

Now, I was really concerned. I ran along the hallway to the cloakroom and pushed open the door. "Estela!" I called again... then suddenly I heard a noise in the day room. I swung around and flung open the door—

"Good morning, Frances."

I knew his voice instantly and as the morning light lit his face, he lifted a jeweled cigar cutter in the air and clipped off the tip of his Havana.

I needed no confirmation... this was a man I could *never* forget.

"Dino?" His name trembled on my lips, reminding me of my terrifying escape from this Mafia godfather.

"Won't you join us for coffee," he said. "You," he pointed towards Estela, who was seated in the corner of the room. "Pour a cup of coffee for my friend."

Estela rose from her chair. She was visibly shaking as she walked towards us, flanked by a Mafioso.

"Indietro!" Dino shouted. "She's not going to run away," he said, mocking his eager newly *made man.*

"I see Gilda still has a photo of my twin brother. The resemblance is uncanny, don't you think?"

I nodded, remembering how I'd mistaken Gilda's late husband for Dino, when I'd first seen it. The twins were identical and once again, I was watching Dino use the jeweled cigar cutter that once belonged to Gilda's husband. I shuddered with the thought of the memory.

My eyes scanned the room and I counted three Mafiosi lurking in the corners. I knew from past experience that there would be others outside and in cars.

"What do you want?" I asked, forcing a smile to placate him. "I'm sure this unannounced early visit is more than a social call."

"Ah, how perceptive of you Frances. I miss your wit and our conversations. But I have to admit that you were not foremost in my mind. I've come to see Gilda," he stated. "And she—" he said pointing to Estela, "*she* claims not to know where she is."

"That's true," I replied and smiled.

Dino was not amused. "My men have searched the house. Where is she?" he demanded.

"Why do you want to see her?" I asked.

"Don't play games with me Frances! You know why... Gilda betrayed us. She and I have unfinished business. Now, tell me where she is?"

"So you have a score to settle?" I asked.

"I'm losing my patience... no more deflections, Frances. Where is she?"

"She's at home," I said.

"In this house?" He sounded astonished.

"Yes," I said.

"Then take me to her."

I walked towards the door. Dino and his Mafiosi followed. "Only you," I said, "leave your goons behind... Gilda can't hurt you now."

I walked along the corridor and stopped in front of a room named, *Le petite chambre*. The fragrance of fresh flowers exploded as I opened the door. A large vase of white lilies was positioned on an antique Tea Table. "Lilies," I said. "Gilda's favorite flowers. Her husband used to have them delivered every week."

"Yeah, I remember. Beni was a good husband, wasn't he Gilda?" Dino walked around the high backed chair, expecting to see the small frame of Gilda, curled up on the cushion. "Frances,… is this some kind'a joke? Where the hell is she?"

"No Dino, this is no joke. It's deadly serious," I said, pointing to a porcelain urn placed on the mantelpiece. "Gilda's last resting place."

The angry expression on Dino's face changed to one of shock.

"You're too late Dino… you can't hurt her now."

Dino looked at the urn and then turned to face me. "She's *dead*?"

"Yes. She died after battling a brain tumor for over a year. The tumor won, but it was a peaceful ending."

Dino stood and thought for a minute. He looked unconvinced. "You're protecting her, aren't you?" he said and grabbed my arm. "Tell me the truth… where is she?"

"Take your hand off me! I told you… she's dead."

"How can I be sure this isn't a trick?" Dino replied.

"You can check with the authorities," I said, "but I have the death certificate." I took an envelope from the mantelpiece, opened it and showed him her name.

Dino sank into the armchair. "She betrayed us, Frances. I never thought Gilda would do that."

"Did you come here to kill her?" I asked.

"I wanted to… it was business, not personal."

"It was *very* personal," I replied. "She was your brother's wife… it can't get much more personal than that!"

"She sold us out! he shouted. "We'll go down for life or rival clans will murder us. She disobeyed Omerta…we're all at risk now!"

"Gilda never took the oath," I said. "It's recorded in the book, that *Omerta* was only for Made Men and higher ranking Mafiosi."

"What? She was a Mafia queen! She *was* high ranking," Dino said in an angry tone.

"But she never took the oath," I told him again. "Because no one asked her to!"

He got up and walked to the window, opened it and inhaled the clear air. "She was clever Frances, like you. She had a way of turning my words around... I lost every damned argument... even this one."

He wandered over to the vase and lifted out a single lily. "You and she are like two lilies from the same stem."

He was more right in his thinking than he knew.

"So you respected her?" I said.

"Of course, but did you really expect me to be lenient? What about the children? Did she think of what might happen to them, when the police arrest their fathers? Right now, every Mafia faction is planning to *hit* us. They all want rid of us because of Gilda... the Mafia queen of the Sorrentino faction. She implicated not only us, but others too. Every faction from Sicily to Bologna is now exposed."

"I think she just wanted the killing to stop," I said in her defense.

"You know what I think, Frances? She wanted to die with a clear conscience," Dino said. "Gilda always had impeccable timing... she's outsmarted me once again. She's up there—," he said, pointing to the ceiling, "laughing at me." he said, shaking his head.

"And me?" I asked. "I transcribed her words. What becomes of me?"

"If the circumstances were different—"

"You mean, if you'd found out about the book before it was published," I said.

"I'll just say... you got lucky—"

"No, it wasn't luck. Gilda planned everything," I interjected. "She took a lesson from her early life... she knew what it felt like to be abused, physically and mentally. She understood that bad behavior survives in secret. She dictated her life story, even though some events were detrimental to herself, and the world is now reading all about it."

"You can't judge us Frances, without judging her too. She practiced revenge, just like us," Dino protested.

"I'm not judgmental, but the public will be. I know only as much as every reader and no more," I replied.

"I suspect you know *far* more. But, remember Frances, you did promise to write my biography, too." Dino looked at me intensely. "I might call in the favor."

"I did, but I doubt yours would be so enlightening."

Dino just smiled. "I guess that's what Gilda would have said, too."

I walked towards the door and held it open. He followed, but paused by the table.

"What's this?" he said, picking up a manuscript. "Another one of your stories?"

"Oh, that?" I said, trying to sound nonchalant. "That's not mine. It was written by my sister. It's her first attempt at writing a novel. It's not very good, in fact it's really awful. And I haven't had the courage to tell her yet." I said.

Dino didn't respond to my explanation and instead began thumbing through the pages. Panic set my heart thumping. "Look, please put it down, I promised her that no one else would read it. "

Dino gave me an intuitive look. "Frances, I feel that this manuscript is more important than you make out."

"I feel obliged to edit it… that's all," I said, as I reached to take it from him.

"Not so fast," he said. "You know that I'm an educated man, don't you Frances?" His eyes glowed with self-confidence as he continued to play his winning hand. "There's a line from Shakespeare and I quote; 'The lady, she doth protest too much.'"

I tried to appease him with a compliment. "I'm aware that you're well-read—"

"And I read *you* now, Frances," he interjected. "There's a reason you don't want me to see this." He held my gaze until I could bear it no more and I turned my head to hide my fear. Dino read aloud the title, "*The Judas Tree…* a story of betrayal. It sounds intriguing."

I didn't answer him…. I knew that further objections would exacerbate the situation. For my own safety, I knew I had to let it go. I also knew that my sister Mary would no longer be protected. She had sent her manuscript labeled for *my eyes only*. Her story described a horrendous episode in her life, which she claimed was true. If her story should become known… then she would be severely punished — or worse.

I escorted Dino to the front entrance, silently berating myself for leaving the manuscript unattended. I never dreamed it would fall into Dino's hands.

"What are your plans, now Gilda is dead?" he asked me.

"I'm not sure," I replied truthfully, as there was now much to consider.

"We have both made mistakes today; I was late and you were careless. We'll speak again… soon." I acknowledged his words with a nod as he walked towards the door.

"Did Gilda have any family?" Dino stopped to ask. "Any relative, hidden away?"

"No, she had no one," I replied.

"Are you sure? Remember Frances, that we hold family responsible. If I should discover a sibling or daughter somewhere, they'll pay for Gilda's treachery," he said.

"Her family are all dead," I said and quickly closed the door.

As Dino walked out to his waiting car, there was a succession of flashes. The press were waiting. They had found Gilda's address and were eager to gain a scoop on the revelations detailed in her book, now that it was published.

One journalist thrust a microphone under Dino's nose. "What's your connection to Gilda and what do you think of her revelations about the Mafia?" he asked.

Dino kept walking. "No comment," he said. His Mafiosi immediately pushed the journalist and TV crews aside, slamming a camera to the ground.

"It's him," one shouted, "he's in the book!"

"Gilda revealed devastating evidence of Mafia brutality..." the reporter's words fed into a microphone and were broadcast live from Carouge.

Dino was now in the car with his Mafiosi violently attacking the accessible cameras trying to capture a photo of a leading Mafia mobster. Their recordings and the live footage would be scooped up and broadcast around the world, much to Dino's disgust.

I watched from the window as he and his mob departed in a convoy, but I counted two less men leaving. I suspected that Dino had ordered two Mafiosi to watch the house, just in case I was lying. The sound of the house telephone interrupted my train of thought.

It was Dino, calling from his car. "Frances, what the hell's going on?"

"The journalists have picked up your scent," I said. "They're after the characters in Gilda's book and you play a leading role. I now have a crowd of TV crews outside the front of the house wanting to know your name. It would probably be wise to recall the two Mafiosi you left behind to watch me," I told him.

"You're very astute Frances... just like Gilda. I'm thinking... that *if only* we could have traded favors, I and you would be saved, and your sister too."

"But, life is full of *if onlys*, isn't it?" I replied.

"Think about this Frances, *if only* I had destroyed Gilda before the book was published and *if only* you'd destroyed the manuscript before I saw it—"

"And if only you hadn't been outed in Gilda's book of revelations," I told him. "The press will have a field day with you, your men and all the people Gilda implicated; the politicians, the police and of course the Mafia...they're all named. There's enough material to keep the FBI busy for years! I don't fancy your chances of survival." I boldly stated.

"Ah, Frances, you underestimate me. You of all people should have learnt from Gilda, that there's a reason why the Sorrentino family has survived for hundreds of years. We're not deterred by dangerous revelations... we *own* Italy. Are you under the illusion that we would relinquish that power now? And all because of a silly book!" he said and the phone went dead.

*

Fate had manifested a karmic reaction. Dino and I were forever changed by the words written in a book and a manuscript. We are both at the mercy of the thoughts and actions of another. Our future is not written in ink... it is written in the blood of our respective families.

My dilemma was obvious. I had to decide whether or not to forewarn my sister of my mishap. She knows nothing of my connection with the Mafia. How would she react when she learnt that her written confession to a bloody crime, is in the hands of the godfather of the most powerful Mafia faction in southern Italy. Who would she fear the most? The police, or the Mafia? It would be a life sentence, whichever way she turned.

Karma is playing a part, just like Gilda prophesied. Our past exchange came back to haunt me now... *'So you're saying that destiny designed the accidents that forged our lives?'* I'd asked her.

'I'm saying that we both know that in life and death, there are no accidents,' Gilda had replied.

I did her a disservice; I withheld two secrets from Gilda while she was alive, which I should have disclosed. The first was that I knew for sure that her son Gary wasn't a murderer. He didn't kill Lauren, but served thirteen long years for a crime he didn't commit. How did I know? My ex-partner Tom, the detective on his case, he knew and withheld that truth from me... for years. He was also responsible for Gary's death, through his careless talk with the Mafia. He asked them to *frighten* Gary, so he'd leave us alone... but instead, they murdered him. The plain truth is that my lover inadvertently killed Gilda's son.

The longer we postpone confessing the truth, the more difficult it becomes. We were building trust through our close relationship and these *secrets* were as thorns in my side, piercing my skin, little by little until the day I would bleed the truth and cleanse my wounds. But that day was pre-empted by Gilda's death and it stole my honesty and now I felt guilty. Was I protecting Gilda or myself? Were karmic forces now in play? Was this my penalty for lying? Although strictly speaking I didn't lie... I only withheld the truth... which is a fine line to draw.

My imagination ran wild and my thoughts were totally illogical.

*

Estela brought in the morning mail. There was a letter from Gilda's lawyer. It stated that I was established as Gilda's next of kin and without doubt a relative of the deceased. But a young American woman, aged eighteen years, also claimed to be a relative. Worse still, she claimed to be Gilda's granddaughter! That would negate my inheritance. I telephoned the lawyer.

"Just because some girl stakes a claim to Gilda's estate, doesn't make it legal," I told him.

"She could well be an imposter," the lawyer replied. "We'd need a DNA test to verify her relationship. I'll investigate further."

I walked up and down the room, fuming at the thought that, possibly, that man ... Gary, who had tried to ruin my life, had conceived a daughter.

It was a double-edged sword. I would definitely benefit from the royalties earned by the sales of the book, but I'd lose the house, its contents and the gold. Then there was Dino to contend with. He would take revenge on the girl, precisely because she's Gilda's relative. She would be in grave danger.

Then, the realization of what could happen became all too clear. If I opposed her claim, it would become a legal matter and public knowledge that I too was a relative. I was overcome with fear at this revelation. I was officially Gilda's cousin... a blood relative.

I had to think fast. Gilda willed her property to me. I was now the rightful owner of this house and its contents and no one except the lawyer knew that I was a relative. This girl could ruin everything!

I returned to the letter Gilda had left me and re-read it. '*The keys and passwords to my deposit boxes are locked in a small safe hidden in the wall, behind the oil painting in my bedroom. I hope you like gold? Just remember my birthday to redeem them.*' How could I have overlooked this?

I rushed upstairs and removed the painting. There in the wall was the safe. I turned the dial in the order of Gilda's date of birth and it opened. Inside were three keys, and each with a specific password and the names of the banks. 'Just like Gilda to spread her assets between banks,' I thought. There was also a cloth bag, which contained a huge amount of cash. A memory came flooding back, '*I also placed some cash inside my home safe, in case I needed to flee,*' she'd told me.

Oh Gilda, you were so well prepared.

It was already mid-morning. The day had started badly. I showered, dressed quickly and left the house. Once inside the first Swiss bank, I was directed to the bank deposit area where I signed in with the clerk. Before she died, Gilda had the foresight to register me as a co-signature in all three banks.   Together the clerk and I entered a secure inner room. All deposit boxes have two keys. She fetched her key, which was registered to my box number, and unlocked one of the locks. With Gilda's key, I unlocked the other and the clerk handed me the box, which I took to a private cubicle. I opened it slowly, not knowing just what I'd find.

There were numerous certificates and the stock was gold… *digital* gold. The amount was staggering! I photographed each certificate and secured the box and called the clerk. We went through the same procedure as before but in reverse.

My next call was at another bank and the procedure was similar. Inside the larger box were not only gold stock certificates, but also diamonds… beautifully cut but unmounted diamonds, along with their individual registrations. Again, I photographed the contents, locked up the box and proceeded to the final bank.

This bank was different. The inside consisted of vaults. After the strict security checks, I was led down into the depths of the building and entered the vaults. There were security checks at every entrance and elevator. I was accompanied by a woman with a pass key.

I was shown into a vault and directed to a door. "This is your room," she told me. I entered and in the center was a mound of gold bars, stacked together. I gasped! I'd never seen gold bars close up before. I leaned forward and touched them… they were smooth and cold. I stood in wonder, walked around the pile and stroked one, as I would a puppy. I tried to lift it, but it was too heavy. 'This was all mine,' I thought and giggled childishly.

I noticed that in the corner of the room, there was a ledger on a small desk. I opened it and read the valuation of the gold. Although the figure would vary with daily trading, overall gold held its price... and that price was phenomenal. This was a significant moment that would have a lasting effect on my life. Here I was in the vault of a Swiss bank with a pile of gold! Who'd have thought it possible! I couldn't have written this in my books and sounded believable.

I sat a while longer, just staring at the gold bars. I relished the luster, and remembered — Gold, symbol Au. atomic number 79.

It was seductive, intoxicating and addictive, with a lifetime's promise of security, influence and control... whenever I should need to utilize it.

Thank you Gilda, I finally understand your love of gold.

Once home, I had much to consider. The house was beautiful and the contents fine, but they were *nothing* compared with the untraceable treasure I now owned. If there really was a granddaughter who had a claim to Gilda's estate, I could share with her... as long as she was legitimate. But the diamonds, the untraceable, untaxable digital gold in the bank deposit boxes, not to mention the vault with the gold bars... *that* was mine to keep.

Gilda was true to her name. Gilde meaning *golden* and the name I'd given her at first sight was... *Goldie.* I now had a secret fortune and I would tell no one. Just like Gilda, I too, knew how to keep a secret.

Shush!— Silence is golden.

THE END

About The Author

Susan Bacoyanis was born and educated in rural England. As an only child she spent many hours alone, developing a vivid imagination that has served her, first as an actor, and now as a writer.

In 2002, Susan moved half way around the world to live and work in California, attending the New York Film Academy and working as a screen actor in Hollywood. She joined the Suzanne DeLaurentiis Productions writing team in Los Angeles, helping establish and promote the Cinema City International Film Festival, which is dedicated to promoting new writers and film makers.

She has published three novels, *There Are No Accidents*, *The Judas Tree* and *Dangerous Revelations*. Further books in the *Linked Series* are planned.

Find out more at: www.susanbacoyanis.com